GW01081425

# THE ANGRY WITCH

## A PONYTEER STORY
### Book One

BY

# T. F. CARROLL

PEN PRESS PUBLISHERS LTD

First published in Great Britain by
Pen Press Publishers Ltd
25 Eastern Place
Brighton
BN2 1GJ

ISBN13: 978-1-906206-25-3

Printed and bound in the UK

A catalogue record of this book is available from
the British Library

Cover design by Alexa Garside

*To my dear grandchildren*
*and children everywhere*
*who enjoy reading a story*

# ACKNOWLEDGEMENT

Thanks to my wife, Joyce, for her constant enthusiasm and patient editing. I think Joyce is truly magical.

# ABOUT THE AUTHOR

## T F Carroll

Thomas Carroll was born in Yorkshire in 1923. He flew in Lancasters during World War II and then retrained as an air traffic controller. After serving for twenty years in the RAF he worked for twenty years in the oil industry. He settled in Cheshire after retirement to be near his grandchildren and his first stories were told to them as bed-time stories until one day they said, "Granddad, why don't you write them down?" – he has been writing ever since!

Also by T F Carroll are books two and three in the Ponyteer trilogy, *The Witches' Revenge* and *Witches on the Run*.

# PART ONE

## THE ROBOTS AND THE WITCH

# CHAPTER ONE

## JUNO AND JUPITER

"Laura, why don't you let Juno show you round the garden?" suggested Professor Klopstock. The professor was referring to the smaller of the two robots that were sitting with him in the lounge, together with Laura and her parents. He waved a hand in the direction of the larger robot, "I want to discuss something with your mum and dad concerning Jupiter, okay?"

"Okay, Professor, I'd love to see your garden," replied Laura. And she really meant it; a look around the garden with Juno was much more interesting to her than listening to a lot of boring old technical and mathematical details. She got out of her chair, "I'm ready when you are, Juno," she said brightly. The robot's metal joints squeaked as she moved over to Laura and, with a little bow, politely offered her an arm. The professor smiled and mumbled good-humouredly into his thick white beard, "I see – no, I hear – our little 'Miss Squeaky Legs' is in good form today."

Everybody smiled at his favourite description of Juno and the robot made a sound that resembled a metallic sort of a laugh. "Pl-ease, co-me wi-th me, Lau-ra." The robot's words were all broken up and sounded strange, but Laura had got used to her way of speaking and could understand her perfectly. She took the robot's arm and together they went through the patio door and stepped out onto a wooden deck.

The professor's house was built on a high hill in San Francisco – the site had been chosen carefully and was ideal for viewing this beautiful city. It was the middle of January, the day was bright and sunny and from their position on the deck, Laura and Juno could see the magnificent Golden Gate Bridge and the abandoned Alcatraz prison squatting low in the water beneath it. With the sun glinting on her metal arms, Juno pointed out many of the places Laura had already visited. Of course, Laura hadn't visited all the places of interest in San Francisco and despite all the months she had lived in the city, she had not yet experienced a ride on their famous streetcars. She was still thinking about this when she heard her mother call out, "Laura, I thought you were going for a walk with Juno?"

"Just going, Mum," Laura called back. She took Juno's hand and together they walked down the wooden steps and into the garden.

When he was sure that Laura was out of earshot the professor said, "I didn't want Laura to be present in case things get acrimonious." He shot a glance at Jupiter, "I can't bear to see children upset." Laura's parents nodded their agreement.

Jupiter, the robot, said nothing but the small red light in the centre of his forehead grew brighter and pulsed more quickly.

Laura and Juno were sitting on a seat in the garden. Juno was doing the talking, "The professor l-ikes calling me 'M-iss Squeaky Legs' – it's a joke we sh-are between us."

"I know," replied Laura, "He really likes you, I can tell."

"But I think Jup-iter's his favourite. He's v-ery proud of him." Juno didn't sound the least bit envious. "Af-ter all," she said, "He's probably the m-ost advanced ro-bot in the w-orld, almost hu-man. Your dad and mum wan-ted him to be the first ro-bot to fly a rocket into outer sp-ace, solo, but Jupit-er says he won't do it."

"Gee, why not, Juno?" Laura could not believe that Jupiter could resist such an opportunity. She said, "I wish I was clever like Jupiter, I'd do it."

"I know. And th-at's the way that your dad and Professor Klop-stock see it." Juno paused. "I reckon they made him too cle-ver, Lau-ra. Their big-gest mistake was to give him a con-science and free wi-ll."

"And now his conscience won't let them spend all that money on the project. He thinks it's a waste. Is that it, Juno?"

"That's right. He says they should find some-thing worthwh-ile to do wi-th their money and not w-aste it on a giant firecracker!"

"Firecracker! Is that what he called it? Phew! I can just see the look on their faces when he called it that."

"It seems fun-ny, I know," said Juno, "But Jupiter soun-ded dead serious when he said that he would rather self-destruct th-an do what they want him to do."

"I don't know Jupiter as well as you, Juno, but I'm pretty sure he wouldn't go that far. Maybe it's just a threat?"

"I don't know," replied the robot, "But there's a l-ot more to Jupit-er than I under-stand. He talks about con-science and free will. I don't really know what conscience a-nd fr-ee will are. In fact I don't know what Jupit-er is talk-ing about most of the time."

3

"And what about the professor, does he know all this is going on in Jupiter's mind?" queried Laura.

"Of course he does, Jup-iter wouldn't kee-p anything from him – ever! He res-pects the professor too much for that and that's why it hurts him – really hurts him – to go against his wishes."

"And it hurts you too, I can see that," said Laura, sympathetically.

Meanwhile, in the house, the professor was beginning to lose patience. "You've been designed specially for this flight, Jupiter. Bill and I have made you so that you've almost become part of us, doesn't that mean anything to you? And the money, the government have a stake in this, don't forget. So don't let us have any more of this nonsense, you've got to do it and that's final!" The professor had grown quite red in the face by the time he had finished.

In contrast to the professor's outburst, Jupiter's reply was perfectly calm. "I don't care. Money, prestige, they mean no-thing to me. Wasting re-sources though, now that's a different mat-ter and my conscience won't all-ow it. All that mon-ey wasted on a giant fire-cracker!" It was amazing how Jupiter made his artificial voice sound derisory when he described the rocket as a giant firecracker. "Why don't you do something w-orth wh-ile with the money?" he said.

The professor exploded, "Giant firecracker! Is that what you call it? You go too far, Jupiter…"

Jupiter interrupted him, "I've got a will of my own. You ga-ve it to me when you made me." Jupiter opened a small flap on his chest and exposed the red self-destruct button. He placed a metal finger on the button. "You gave me l-ife, Professor, but you also gave me the means of des-troying it. Please don't m-ake me use it."

4

The professor looked around and saw the robot immobiliser on the table. His mind was made up. No more pussyfooting around. He would immobilise Jupiter and, with Bill's help, make a few adjustments that would erase all this silly nonsense about free will from Jupiter's mind forever! Bill saw the professor looking at the immobiliser and instantly read his thoughts. When the professor raised his eyes to him he nodded his approval. They were in this together.

Down in the garden it was beginning to get misty. San Francisco is like that sometimes; one minute bright sunshine and then, in the next minute, mist rolling in. Laura felt a shiver run through her body. "We'll have to go in soon, Juno, it's getting a bit chilly," she murmured. Looking at Juno for an answer, she noticed the dull red light centred in Juno's forehead had intensified and was flickering about in an alarming fashion. Juno leapt to her feet. "D-anger! D-anger! Invest-igate! Invest-igate!"

Her voice was loud and anxious and more broken up than ever. "St-ay in the g-arden. Stay in the g-arden, Laura. D-anger! D-anger!" She continued to shout the warning as she bounded up the wooden steps to the house.

Juno's sense of impending danger was real, but she was too late to avert the disaster about to follow. As she got to the patio door she saw the professor reach out for the immobiliser, which lay on the table. Jupiter realized what was happening and tried to get there before him but tripped over a rug and fell forward onto the table. Laura's parents' eyes opened wide in horror when they saw that the flap on the self-destruct button was still open. The button was depressed the moment Juno fell onto the table and the self-destruct system was set into motion.

The professor and the robot's eyes met over the table. The anger in the professor's eyes had been replaced by a look of intense sadness. He said quietly, "Dear Jupiter, what have you done?"

Jupiter's reply was equally sad, "F-orgive me, Professor, it w-as an accident. I n-ever intended to d-estroy the life that you had created."

The professor reached out to touch Jupiter's hand. As their fingers met, a violent explosion rocked the room and a shower of metal that had once been Jupiter was hurled with deadly force in all directions. Laura's parents were killed instantly and the professor was barely alive when the rescuers came and carried him out. Juno was flung backwards onto the wooden deck looking like a tangled piece of scrap metal. The red light in the centre of her forehead pulsed so faintly, it could hardly be seen.

On hearing the explosion, Laura leapt out of her seat in the garden and ran up the steps towards the house, where she saw Juno lying in a heap on the deck, all bent and twisted. Crying and barely coherent she ran to the neighbours next door to get help.

The shock of her parents' death and of the professor's serious injuries made Laura very ill and she spent weeks and weeks recovering in a San Francisco hospital. During this time her grandparents visited her, but Laura was too ill to be moved and they returned to England without her.

Laura repeatedly asked her doctors and nurses about the professor's recovery, only to be told that he was making slow progress. When she asked about Juno, all she got in return were blank stares, "Juno, who on earth is Juno?" Juno had disappeared without trace and nobody seemed to care.

The month of June arrived and Laura was strong enough to push the professor's wheelchair into the hospital garden and there they sat talking together, sometimes for over an hour. Their friendship deepened and soon she found she could talk about her parents without weeping.

The professor was a great storyteller and Laura was fascinated when he recounted to her some of his World War II exploits. She was surprised and interested to learn that he was an archaeologist long before he became famous as a rocket scientist.

After the war the professor decided to spend a short time in England before returning to the States. He grew to like England so much he stayed on for five whole years!

Laura asked him where he had lived whilst he was in England. "Chester," he said, "although when the Romans occupied it they called it Deva. Did you know that, Laura?"

"No," said Laura, "but Grandma and Granddad live near Chester, so I expect they'll tell me all about that when I go to live with them."

The professor's face lit up when he heard the news. "Chester, really? That's interesting. Whereabouts near Chester?"

Laura told him she would be staying in the small village of Tinsall, which was about eight miles from the city.

"Well, I'll be darned," said the professor, tugging excitedly at his beard. "That's where I made some of my most important digs. Now where exactly was it? Tinsall Hill, yes, that's it, that's the place. Now, there was a little café on the hill I used to visit. If only I could remember its name…" His face had quite a dreamy look about it.

"Could it be the Tea Pot Café? I've heard Grandma and Granddad talk about a café with that name."

"That's it! Well, I'll be darned. So it's still there after all these years?"

Whilst Laura was wheeling him back to his ward he talked about two prototype robots he had made in Cheshire many years ago. "Like clockwork toys really, compared to those your dad and I made, Laura. Do you know what I named them?"

Without pausing to think, Laura replied, "Juno and Jupiter Junior." And she was absolutely right about that.

By late July, Laura was making a good recovery and her grandparents came to collect her and take her back with them to England. Before leaving the hospital, she introduced them to the professor. They found him sitting in a wheelchair in the hospital garden, reading. Over the top of his book the professor caught them eyeing the bandaged stump of his right leg. Laura's grandparents were embarrassed and looked away.

"Don't worry, folks, they're giving me a new metal leg soon and then it will be Juno's turn to call *me* Squeaky Legs!" The professor sounded cheerful. Laura was so excited she could hardly breathe.

"Juno! Professor, you've seen her? Is she alright?"

"No, I haven't seen her. But let's put it this way, if Juno's disappeared without trace, then she's alive, and if she's alive, she's quite capable of repairing herself. I expect she'll turn up and surprise me when I get out of hospital."

He caught Laura looking at the black patch over his eye and chuckled, "Yes, it's still there, Laura, but don't worry, I won't have to look like a pirate for much longer, the sight in my eye can be saved. It'll look a bit scarred mind you, but at least I'll be able to see again."

Grandma and Granddad stood up. They said it was time to go. The professor pressed a large bulky envelope into Laura's hands. "Here you are, my dear. My present to the bravest girl in the world."

"A present? Gee, thanks Professor. What is it?" she asked, before she could stop herself, and she felt her cheeks

8

burn red with embarrassment. "Sorry, I shouldn't have asked…"

"No, my child, you're quite right to ask. It's my fault really. I should have told you the whole story before I offered it to you." The professor turned towards Laura's grandparents. "It's not a long story, do you have time to listen?"

Mr Stuart looked at his watch. "Well, we have some papers to sign at the hospital before we leave. How about we do that and wait for Laura in reception?" He looked at his watch again, "Our taxi leaves for the airport in 20 minutes. That time enough for you?"

"We'll be through by then."

"Okay then, Jules," said Mr Stuart, addressing the professor by his first name. "Goodbye, my friend, and thanks for all you've done for Laura. See you in England – one day soon – we hope."

"You can bank on it," replied the professor.

Grandma Stuart bent and gave Laura a kiss on the cheek, "See you in reception, Laura."

"Okay, see you, Gran."

When all the waving and goodbyes were over, Professor Klopstock started his story:

"One day when I was out on one of my digs on Tinsall Hill, I discovered a Roman treasure cave. It was almost packed from floor to ceiling with precious objects – fantastic! I meant to tell the local museum curators about my find, but kept putting it off, thinking I would tell them when I had finished my exploration on the hill. Then I was suddenly recalled to the States where I became involved with some very important work for my country and I've been so immersed in this work that I completely forgot about the treasure, until you mentioned Tinsall and Chester and then it all came back to me. That's the story; it's as simple as that. And that envelope, Laura, contains a map and my journal, which shows exactly where the treasure is hidden."

Laura's face was flushed with excitement. "Wow! A treasure map! A real treasure map? Tell me it's real, Professor."

"It's real, Laura. Sure is. But wait, I haven't finished yet. First, I must impress upon you the importance of reading my journal. Remember to read it carefully before you set out to seek the treasure, otherwise you could end up in trouble. Okay?"

"Okay Professor, I will read it carefully. Promise."

"Good, and when you find the treasure, I know you will make sure it's taken to the museum, where it rightfully belongs."

"Oh, I will, I will."

An anxious note crept into the professor's voice, "My final word is a word of warning, Laura, and I want you to listen carefully because it is very important." He looked at Laura from under his bushy eyebrows and asked, "Are you listening to me, Laura?"

"Yes, sir, I'm listening very carefully."

"Good. Now when you look at the map you will see 'DANGER AREA' etched on it in red. The locals call it 'the dark side of the hill' and they will tell you that nothing has grown on it for over 50 years! I enquired about it but no one seems to know why. It's a mystery. There's just one more thing you ought to know and then I'm finished. It's about that danger area. Now, Laura, are you ready for the big one?"

Laura nodded; she was too excited to speak.

"Tinsall Hill is almost completely hollow. I discovered this when I was carving my initials on a sandstone rock to mark where I had found the treasure cave. I heard screaming and shouting going on *under* the hill, like there was a battle in progress…"

"You mean there are people living there, Professor? What sort of people could they be living under the hill? Did you see them?"

"No, I didn't see them. But I heard them all right, and pretty nasty they sounded too: fierce, warlike – dangerous! I was recalled to the States before I could find out more. You must promise me, Laura, that you will keep away from the dark side of the hill."

Laura nodded, "Bet your life I will."

"So, the treasure map, Laura, now you've heard the story, do you still want it?"

"More than ever," replied Laura.

"Brave girl," said the professor. "I thought that you would. Take care though, and good luck with the treasure hunt."

After a final hug, Laura went to join her grandparents at the hospital reception desk. They left almost immediately for San Francisco airport, where they boarded a plane for England.

Laura told her grandparents about the Roman treasure map but thought it best if she kept the professor's warning about the dark side of the hill to herself, in case it made them feel anxious for her safety.

She tried to get some sleep on the long air journey to London, but whenever she closed her eyes she imagined the creatures living under the hill. They were small and fierce and guarding the Roman treasure cave. The door to the cave was open and she could see a vast hoard of gold and silver treasure lying in scattered heaps upon the floor, but when she tried to go through the door to reach it, those fierce creatures screamed and shouted at her and chased her away with sharp-looking swords…

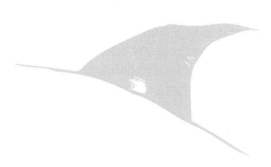

# CHAPTER TWO

## BAD NEWS FOR LEANNE,
## LINDSEY AND ALISON

In the village of Tinsall the two sisters, Leanne and Lindsey Farroll, were preoccupied with problems of their own. Compared to the nightmare Laura was having on the flight from San Francisco to England, Leanne and Lindsey's worries were of a very practical nature. "What do you want first, the good news or the bad news?" asked their granddad when he came into the living room accompanied by the children's parents. "The good news, the good news, Granddad," chorused Leanne and Lindsey.

Granddad turned to his son, smiled and said, "Told you they'd want the good news first, Chris, didn't I?"

"Please, please, Granddad." Two shining faces with wide-open eyes looked up at Granddad expectantly.

"Oh, all right then, so here's the news you've been waiting for – Laura is on her way to England – Granddad and Grandma Stuart are travelling on the plane with her. They'll be arriving at Heathrow today."

Leanne and Lindsey were overjoyed at the news; to have a brand new friend coming all the way from America was exciting enough, but San Francisco? They couldn't wait to see Laura – San Francisco was something special.

When the excitement had died down, Lindsey asked, "So, what's the bad news, Granddad?"

Lindsey's granddad hesitated. "Well, it is bad news, I suppose. But it's nothing that can't be put right, Lindsey. So don't you and Leanne start worrying. Your dad and me, we'll sort it out, won't we Chris?"

"Yes, Dad, we will."

"But what is the bad news, Granddad?" Leanne asked. "Is it something we ought to know?"

Again Granddad hesitated…

"Best if you tell them, Dad. If you don't, they'll only worry," said Leanne's father.

"'Spect you're right, Son," said Granddad and he began to tell the girls what the bad news was. "Remember that land I sold to the Stuarts, you know, when they first arrived in the village?"

Leanne and Lindsey nodded.

"Well, now Laura's coming to live with them, they want to extend the cottage and make it a lot bigger. Make everything modern, you know? And in order to do that they'll have to knock down the outbuildings…"

"And the stables where our ponies, Poppy and Peace, are stabled, too. That's it, isn't it, Granddad? That's the bad news," said Lindsey, and crying, she ran to her room upstairs.

"I'll go after her," said her mother. "She's upset. You come with me, Leanne, help me to persuade Lindsey that everything will be alright."

Although Leanne and Lindsey were assured by their dad and mum that new accommodation would be found for their ponies, they couldn't help feeling miserable and phoned their friend Alison, whose father owned a riding school, hoping she would know about some alternative stabling.

Alison, however, had worries of her own. She told them that her father was very angry about her pony, Flikka, who, for some unaccountable reason, had started to kick out at everyone who dared to come near him. Some customers were afraid of him and had taken their business elsewhere. Alison said that her dad had warned her that she had got just two weeks to teach her pony Flikka not to kick out at everyone, otherwise he would have to go. Tearfully, she told the girls that her father was so angry he had said that she should have called her pony Kikka, not Flikka!

"I'm going out with Flikka now," she said. "When we are on our own, perhaps I can talk some sense into him and change him back into the friendly pony that he used to be. Ring you later and tell you how I get on."

Alison tucked her mobile away and rode out through the riding school gates and into the country lanes. She leaned forwards in the saddle to stroke Flikka's ears. "What's happening to you, Flikka?" she said, "You used to be such a happy pony, flicking your tail about whenever anyone spoke to you. That's why I named you Flikka, don't you remember?"

Flikka snorted. "Good," said Alison, "You seem to remember that. Well now, may I ask you to please stop kicking out at people, please Flikka, please."

Flikka snorted again. "Hmm," said Alison, "I hope that means you're going to behave, because at the bottom of his heart dad really doesn't want to let you go. But you are ruining his business, Flikka, and if you don't change your nasty habits he'll be forced into doing something he really doesn't want to do. And... and try to think about me, for a change. Think how unhappy it will make me if they send you away."

Flikka lifted up his head and whinnied. Alison did not have time to find out whether the whinny meant "yes" he would change his habits, or "no" he wouldn't, because a fox suddenly darted across the road in front of them. Flikka was so startled he leapt high in the air. His legs were stiffened with fear and when he came down again the sudden jolt sent poor Alison crashing headlong into a ditch. She lay there dazed and moaning with pain, while Flikka, still startled by the fox, turned quickly and galloped away.

Fortunately, Leanne and Lindsey had decided to ride their ponies, Poppy and Peace, along the same route that had been taken by Alison. Lindsey spotted something on the road. "Look," she cried, pointing; "Isn't that Alison's riding crop?"

Their worries forgotten, Leanne and Lindsey jumped down from their ponies and went to investigate. Sure enough, the riding crop they saw was one that belonged to Alison. After a careful search of the area they found Alison lying in a ditch almost hidden by grass and weeds.

"Oh, poor Alison. Look, Lindsey, she must have been thrown there by Flikka." Both girls slid down into the ditch to see what they could do to help. They touched her gently, examining her. She felt cold and looked very pale. The sisters took off their riding jackets and laid them over Alison, rubbing her hands to warm them.

"She needs a doctor, Lindsey," whispered Leanne. "But we must try and keep her as warm as we can until we get some help."

"Shall we try and carry her out of the ditch?" said Lindsey.

"No, that might do more harm than good."

"What shall we do then, ride back to the stables and tell her dad?"

"No. Take too much time, Lindsey. In any case Mr Rawlins might not be home and we can't leave poor Alison lying here in the ditch alone."

"What then?" said Lindsey; she was still rubbing Alison's hands.

"There's only one thing for it," said Leanne decisively. "I'll take a short cut over the fields to Doctor Harris's house; it's her day off and she'll be spending all her time in the garden. Well, that's what she told Granddad yesterday."

Lindsey was looking anxious. "Don't worry, Lindsey," said Leanne, putting an arm round her sister and giving her a hug. "I'm confident that Peace can clear all of the gates and hedges, I don't think that she'll let me fall off."

"You sure?" said Lindsey, with a tremor in her voice.

"Absolutely," said Leanne, as she leapt into the saddle. "You look after Alison, Lindsey, 'til I get back with Doctor Harris, okay?" And without another word Leanne and Peace were off like the wind to fetch the doctor.

"Okay, Leanne, I'll look after Alison," called Lindsey, but Leanne was already too far away to hear.

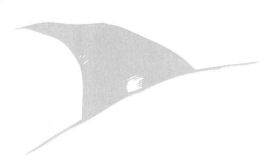

# CHAPTER THREE

## RESCUE AND REWARD

Although Lindsey had been left alone with Alison for only a very short time, it seemed like an age to her. The sun was low in the sky now and she shivered, it was beginning to get cold. She tucked the riding jackets even closer around Alison, whose eyelids flickered, opened briefly and closed again. Then Alison moaned. "It's all right, Alison, it's me, don't be frightened, Leanne's gone to get Doctor Harris and I'm staying right here with you until they come back." Lindsey continued to rub Alison's hands to try to bring some heat into them and every now and again she would squeeze them gently, to reassure Alison that she had somebody with her who cared.

Fortunately for Leanne, the hedges had been recently cut and she was able to clear most of them with several inches to spare. Peace was magnificent, she seemed to understand the seriousness of the situation and was determined to do her best to help. As she sailed over hedges and gates she snorted loudly as if to say, "See, Leanne, you can rely on me."

Doctor Harris's eyes opened wide with astonishment when Peace came flying over her hedge and landed in the garden quite close to where she was working. Leanne tethered Peace and then followed the doctor into the house, explaining what had happened and describing to the doctor where she could expect to find Lindsey and Alison.

In next to no time Doctor Harris was ready. She flung her medical bag into the car and settled into the driving seat but, before starting the engine, she wound down her window and advised Leanne to take the easy way back. "Go the long way round, show jumping's over for today and you know something, Leanne – you really are the best!" Leanne relaxed and gave the doctor a wave; she knew Alison would soon be in safe hands.

By the time Leanne returned to the scene of the accident, Doctor Harris had already diagnosed the extent of Alison's injuries and, assisted by Lindsey, she had laid her safely on the back seat of the car.

Alison had not yet regained full consciousness and the doctor decided to take her to hospital for tests. She gave the girls some instructions, "Tell Alison's mum and dad they can find us in the casualty department, Countess of Chester Hospital. Alison doesn't appear to be seriously hurt but it would be best to have a thorough check up."

"We'll tell them, Doctor Harris, as quickly as we can. We'll try to phone them first." Leanne patted her pocket to make sure her mobile phone was still there.

"Just one last thing before I go, I'm really proud of you two girls," the doctor said. "So brave and so *responsible*. You both deserve a gold medal!" She put the car into gear and drove away to the hospital leaving Leanne and Lindsey blushing with embarrassment. With those words of praise still ringing in their ears, they phoned Alison's parents to tell them what had happened.

At the end of a long tiring day, the sisters were ready for an early bedtime. They were about to climb the stairs when the doorbell rang; Alison's mum and dad had come to tell the good news that Alison was not seriously injured and would be discharged from hospital the very next day. Mr Rawlins looked grave when he said, "But that's all thanks to these young ladies. If they hadn't found Alison and helped…" Overcome by emotion, he paused for a moment, then said, "Our poor Alison, she might have been very ill, very ill indeed" Mrs Rawlins put her arm round him and comforted him.

"What about Flikka?" asked Lindsey, boldly posing the question.

"Oh, he's alright," said Mr Rawlins, "Came trotting in through the gates a couple of hours ago looking very sorry for himself."

All this welcome news brought about a lot of hugging and kissing and even a few tears were shed, especially when Mr and Mrs Rawlins again thanked Leanne and Lindsey for saving Alison. When things had calmed down a bit, Mr Rawlins said that he had heard they were having problems in stabling Poppy and Peace and if it was okay with Mr and Mrs Farroll, they could have free stabling at the riding school for just as long as they wished. Mr Farroll stuttered out his acceptance and the two men then shook hands. Mrs Farroll and Mrs Rawlins hugged one another, making it plain to the girls that they would soon become close friends.

The next day, Leanne and Lindsey took the ponies to their new stables and as they were shown into the paddock, Flikka trotted to greet them. Nuzzling up to Peace he flicked his tail to show how much he liked her. And then something almost magical happened; Flikka became calm and contented again, just as he had been before. There was no more kicking out from Flikka now; he became docile and friendly as could be. But then, how could he be otherwise, when he had a companion who was gentle as Peace?

Word got around about the remarkable change in Flikka's nature and with his good name now restored, business improved quickly at the stables for Mr Rawlins. Mr Rawlins was thinking about that as he swept up the stable yard. But the best news of all that entered his mind was that Alison's accident had left her unharmed. Now she was recovering well and seemed as strong as ever.

When Doctor Harris told the story about the bravery of Leanne and Lindsey to her friends, one of them must have mentioned it to Mr Gribe, the local newspaper reporter. "Gribe The Scribe" as he was affectionately called, devoted the whole of his weekly column to the story and he had pictures of the girls printed alongside his column. Overnight, Leanne and Lindsey became famous.

Alison was out of hospital riding Flikka again and Leanne and Lindsey were enjoying riding their ponies with her. All their parents watched as the girls practised jumps over hurdles in the paddock.

"It's a miracle," said Alison's dad. "The change in that pony is nothing short of a miracle, he never gets angry and never kicks out and it's all thanks to Peace."

"No, my dear," said Mrs Rawlins, correcting her husband, gently. "In my opinion it's all due to Leanne and Lindsey, without their help our Alison would never have got to hospital in time and – and…" her voice trailed off. She wiped away a tear before she continued, "And, and without their help, Flikka would be called Kikka! And just look at him now, did you ever see such a friendly pony?"

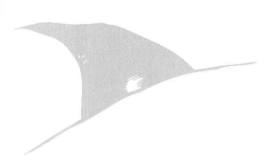

# CHAPTER FOUR

## LINDSEY TELLS WHAT SHE'S HEARD ABOUT LAURA

On a fine sunny morning in the middle of the school summer holidays, Leanne and Lindsey, with their friend Alison, were standing on the tree house platform enjoying the views all around. They were high enough up to see what was going on in the riding school at the bottom of the hill and they watched as Alison's parents busied themselves in the stable yard.

"Dad says business has never been as good," said Alison. "All the old customers who left have come back and we've got lots of new ones as well."

"My dad says you must have gained some new customers because of Mr Gribe's column in the local newspaper. He recommended that Peace and Flikka, frolicking around together in the paddock, was a sight that no one should miss."

"I know," said Alison, "Mr Gribe helped a lot." The girls sighed contentedly. After all the bad news things now seemed to be looking very much brighter.

Leanne shielded her eyes against the sun as she looked into the distance. Beyond the riding school she could clearly see the outline of the Welsh mountains. She thought that as they rose high into the sky they resembled a sleeping giant whose outstretched arms were protecting the whole of the Cheshire plain. The winter snow had melted months ago and now the mountains were coloured in varied shades of green and brown. A solitary cloud moved across the sunlit sky casting its shadow on the ground and creating fleeting patterns of shade and light on everything that it touched.

Leanne lowered her gaze in the direction of the stable yard and noticed that Mr Rawlins was doing something to one of the horse's hooves. "What's your dad doing, Alison?" she asked. "What's that he's pouring into the horse's hoof?"

"Oh, that's Mr Slaughter's horse, Bosey," said Alison. "He's just had an abscess lanced by the vet. My dad's giving Bosey special treatment to make sure that his hoof is clean and clear of infection."

From their vantage position on the tree house they watched Mr Rawlins until he had finished his treatment on the hoof. "Ugh," said Lindsey, "I bet that abscess left a nasty hole there."

Alison said, "Yes, but it will soon heal if it's kept clean and clear of infection."

"Ooh, just listen to Alison," said Lindsey, "I think she'd make a marvellous vet. Is that what you would like to be?"

"Hmm. Maybe," said Alison and they knew by the way she said it that she really did want to be a vet.

Changing the subject, Lindsey said, in a voice as nonchalant as she could, "I heard Mum and Dad talking about the Stuarts and Laura last night."

"Oh, did you," said Leanne. "Well, you know what they say about little pigs, don't you?"

"Do you want to know what they were talking about, or not," Lindsey snapped.

"Oh, all right, let's hear it then, come on Linz, I was only teasing."

"Oh, c'mon, Lindsey, don't be like that," said Alison. "Beats me why Laura's coming to live in boring old Tinsall anyway. Well, it's not like America, is it? Doesn't Laura know that this is the village where nothing ever happens?"

There was a tremor in Lindsey's voice as she began to speak. "Laura's coming to live in Tinsall because her mum and dad got killed, that's why." Her voice had fallen to a whisper by the time she reached the end of her sentence.

The news was so shocking, it took quite a few seconds before Leanne was able to speak, "Oh, Lindsey, Lindsey, how awful. Where were they killed? How did it happen?"

"The accident happened in San Francisco. Her mum and dad were working with professor somebody or other on a robot called Jupiter when it exploded. It killed Laura's mum and dad and badly injured the professor."

"And Laura, what about Laura?" asked Leanne, anxiously.

"Laura wasn't injured in the blast, because the explosion happened in the house and she was in the garden. But she was ages and ages in hospital in America before she got over the shock. The Stuarts say they hear her crying sometimes when she's in bed at night. Anyway, the good thing is, Laura said she would like to meet us and the Stuarts think that would help, but she should have a few more days rest first."

"Poor Laura," the girls muttered. Overwhelmed by the sad news they were reduced to silence.

Leanne was the first to recover her voice, "How is it?" she asked Lindsey, "how is it that you heard all this and I didn't?"

" 'Cos you were asleep and I was on the stairs listening, that's why," said Lindsey, and she had a "beat that if you can" look spread across her face.

Leanne didn't bother to respond. She thought that Laura's story was too sad to squabble over.

All this tragic news had reminded Alison again about her own accident. "When you add together all those terrible things that have happened to Laura and also what happened to me, it makes you realize that there must be a lot of people who need all kinds of help. I'd like to help if I could. Do you feel the same way about it as me?

Both Leanne and Lindsey responded enthusiastically.

"But if we're offering to help people," Lindsey said, "then we've got to have a name, otherwise how will people know who to come to when they want help?"

"What about the Three Ponyteers?" suggested Leanne, remembering the title of the film *The Three Musketeers* she had seen on TV.

Alison and Lindsey agreed that it was a great name for a group that was prepared to ride out to help people.

Alison said she would stencil THE PONYTEERS in bright colours on their white tee shirts.

"Now, what about a motto? The Musketeers had one," Lindsey said.

"You've thought of one already, Linz, I can tell by the sound of your voice," said Leanne, casting a knowing look at her sister.

Lindsey blushed and hesitated. "I had thought of one," she said, scraping the toe of her shoe on the floor, "But I don't think that you'll like it."

"Do you want to die, little fly?" said Alison, advancing on Lindsey and putting a most frightening expression on her face.

"Okay, okay, Alison, don't kill me, I'll tell," said Lindsey. "But if you laugh at me, I'll never speak to either of you again!"

Alison and Leanne solemnly agreed not to laugh. Reassured, Lindsey stood up and recited:

*If you need any help, or if you are afraid,*
*Call the Three Ponyteers and they will come to your aid.*

She sat down looking self-conscious. For a few seconds there was silence and then Leanne and Alison shouted, "Brilliant! That's our new motto, Lindsey. That's it! That's it!"

Before they went home the girls printed a notice and stuck it on the tree house door. It read "Headquarters, The Three Ponyteers".

When Alison returned the next day she brought the new tee shirts with her and they darted up to Leanne's bedroom to try them on. When they came out of the house wearing them they were beaming with delight.

They were still admiring their tee shirts when they heard peals of loud laughter and shouting. "Boys," sniffed Lindsey, "Why are they always so noisy?"

"Sounds like our Alex with his pal, Ginger Tomkins," said Leanne, "They're always laughing and yelling like that. No use telling them to quieten down, they'll only make more noise than ever."

Alex and Ginger Tomkins were outside the house now and Alex was yelling goodbye to his chum, Ginger, at the top of his voice. Every time Alex called "goodbye" Ginger came back with a call that was even louder. After a while they got tired of shouting and Ginger went home.

Alex came into the garden and sat down beside them. He looked dishevelled. Lindsey turned her nose up at him, "You look scruffy. Why don't you go inside and take a bath, I could smell you a mile away!" Lindsey was annoyed, she had been enjoying the "all girls together" talk before her brother had arrived on the scene and she knew that it was only a matter of time before he would spoil it.

But Alex wasn't pleased either. Who did Lindsey think she was, telling him he was scruffy and smelly and needing a bath? He scowled at the girls. "I've been playing football, and you'd look scruffy if you'd been playing football on a muddy field." Then his scowl was replaced by a beaming smile, "Our team won one-nil, if you want to know. And guess who scored the winning goal – go on have a guess?"

"You, Alex," said Lindsey, wearily. "You scored the winning goal."

"Dead right, Lindsey," said Alex, and he was about to describe this wonderful achievement when he noticed the new tee shirts the girls were wearing.

"I want one of those," he demanded.

"Well you can't," said Lindsey, peevishly. "You don't have a pony. You can't ride a pony. You're not the least bit interested in ponies and you don't help at the stables, so you can't be a Ponyteer. And if you're not a Ponyteer you can't have a tee shirt like us and that's final, so there!"

"Well, I'll go to the stables then if I get a shirt like that. I'm going to be a Ponyteer, Lindsey, you can't stop me."

Leanne sensed that angry tears were not far away. "Hold on a minute, Alex. What do you think about this for an idea? Suppose Alison gets you a tee shirt and we make you an honorary Ponyteer. What do you think about that?"

In truth it was only the shirt that Alex wanted, he didn't care about belonging to the group, but the word "honorary" intrigued him; he hadn't heard that word before. He made three silent attempts to say the word before he thought he had got it right, and then slowly, and with some suspicion, he asked, "What's honorary?"

Leanne explained, "Honorary Ponyteer means that you can wear a special Ponyteer tee shirt and attend all the meetings – but only if you want to. And it means you don't have to do any work at the stables – if you don't want to." Leanne saw her brother's face beginning to relax – no tears threatening now! Then, with a touch of inspiration, she added, "It means that football always comes first."

Alex got out of his chair feeling very satisfied. "Alright then, Leanne, I'll be an honorary Ponyteer." He puffed out his chest and strutted into the house to explain to his mum what an honorary Ponyteer was and how he had scored the winning goal for his team.

"Phew!" breathed Alison with relief, "I thought he was going to throw one of his tantrums!"

"You've got to remember that Alex is very young," said Leanne quietly. "But if you talk gently and persuasively to him, he can easily be diverted."

"That's true," said Lindsey, "But sometimes I forget about that and I shout at him like mad. Then I feel mean when I've done it and have to say sorry to him."

"Forget about Alex for a minute, will you?" said Leanne. "This motto of ours, we know what it means and what we want to do. But no one else in the village even knows that the Ponyteers exist, do they? So how are we to tell them?"

"Advertise," said Lindsey, brightly.

"Where, how, Lindsey?"

"I dunno, I just suggested it, that's all."

"We could do leaflets, put them through letterboxes," said Alison.

"Take too long," said Leanne. "No, I think we should ask Mr Slaughter to stick a poster up in his shop. Everybody visits the butchers. Within a few days everybody will have seen it."

Alison and Lindsey agreed this was a great idea and set to work to design a very eye-catching poster to take along to Mr Slaughter's shop.

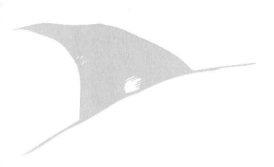

# CHAPTER FIVE

WITCH EASTLY PLOTS TO FOIL
THE PONYTEERS' PLANS

Mr Slaughter recognised Alison the moment she walked in the shop. "Good job your dad did on my Bosey, Alison, he's as fit as a fiddle now." He spotted the poster that she was carrying in her hands. "What's that you've got there, young lady, not hiding something from me, are you?"

"No, it's something to show you, Mr Slaughter," said Alison. She handed the poster to him and explained what the Ponyteers hoped to do. Mr Slaughter was impressed. He placed the poster in the most prominent position available.

All the customers who came into Mr Slaughter's shop read the Ponyteers' motto with genuine sounds of approval – except one! It was Mrs Eastly; she did not like the motto at all. Nobody in the village knew it, but Mrs Eastly was really an old witch who liked her own motto best, which was, "Never do good, and whatever you've read, give evil a chance and do evil instead!"

When Mrs Eastly left the butcher's shop she was

determined to plot a scheme that would foil the Ponyteers' good intentions.

Mrs Eastly lived with her twin stepsons in Red House Farm, which lay about one mile from the centre of the village. She sat in her den with her mind full of evil thoughts, trying to devise the plan that would hurt the Ponyteers most. In the end she decided that the best plan would be to steal their ponies. Without ponies they would have to abandon all their promises to do good works. It was a wicked thought but it appealed to her twisted sense of humour. Her lips parted in a sneering grin, which showed all her yellow jagged teeth. With a growl of satisfaction she vowed her battle against the Ponyteers was just about to begin.

Stealing the ponies would not be a problem for Mrs Eastly. She could easily force her twin stepsons to do that, but in order to carry out the plan successfully they would need all the relevant information. For example, they would have to know exactly where the ponies were being stabled, and have an exact description of them, it was important to know that. Mrs Eastly didn't want the boys to steal somebody else's ponies by mistake; that's why she was working so hard on the plan. And at the stables would the ponies be in their stalls or in the paddock? She discounted the idea that they would be out to pasture for two reasons. One, the hedge cutters were in the area making a lot of noise and their machinery could frighten the ponies. Two, there was building work at the Stuarts' cottage and Mrs Eastly felt almost sure the animals would be kept safely indoors.

She decided to reconnoitre the area that very night in order to provide all the answers she needed.

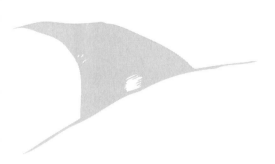

# CHAPTER SIX

## WITCH EASTLY TAKES TO THE AIR

Mrs Eastly was a poor performer on the broomstick. Some witches, who knew a thing or two about flying broomsticks, said that she was downright incompetent. She hadn't much confidence in her own flying capabilities, either. She took no chances with the weather; it had to be just right before she would even attempt to get airborne. All her sister witches knew that. Behind her back they scoffed at her and called her "Big Bertha, the fair weather broomstick flier!"

Before taking off to explore the area where the ponies were stabled, Mrs Eastly stepped outside the house and made a careful check on the weather. It was a cloudless night, with just a sliver of a moon and the whisper of a breeze; it was ideal weather for broomstick flying. The moon gave sufficient light to enable Mrs Eastly to see where she was going; yet it remained dark enough to make it difficult for others to see her. The witch donned her long black cloak and her black pointed hat which in the dark, made her almost invisible. She took one last pre-flight check on her broomstick, to make sure that the flight operating button was at the correct setting for takeoff, and then she was ready.

Mrs Eastly made a strong push-off with her stout, sturdy legs. Her bony fingers found the operating button and slid it forward into climbing position; the broomstick responded and went up into a gentle climb. Feeling nervous, Bertha decided to make the flight low and slow. She eased back the flight-operating button to the central position before she had reached the height of 20 metres and the broomstick immediately adopted a straight and level flying attitude. Swaying her body slightly she turned her broomstick on, heading for the riding school. "Just like riding a bike," she cackled. Bertha was beginning to feel more confident.

She did not time the flight, but it must have taken only three or four minutes before she was hovering overhead the riding school "Not bad for an old fashioned model," she said, patting her magic broomstick affectionately.

She peered down at the ground below. "Too high," she said to herself. "I'll do a couple of low-level circuits around the paddock first, just to see if the ponies are there, then I'll decide what my next move will be." A slight adjustment on the flight operational button was all that was needed to take her to exactly the height she wanted. She scanned the paddock in the feeble moonlight, searching for the ponies. Just as she thought, they were not there; they must be in their stalls.

A large tree growing in the middle of the paddock suddenly loomed up ahead, and she had to lean over at an extreme angle to avoid flying into it. She had made a violent manoeuvre and almost fell off her broomstick. Her heart beat wildly. "Concentrate, Bertha. Concentrate!" she chided herself severely. It had been a very narrow escape and her hands were still shaking as she moved the flight operational button to the number one position. Her idea now was to make a gentle landing in the centre of the stable yard. It should have been easy, but Mrs Eastly's flying skills were poor and her timing was wrong. The broomstick stopped flying when she was still a good metre in the air and she crashed heavily onto the ground. The impact threw her off her broomstick and for a few moments she lay there all winded and bruised. The witch winced with pain as she staggered to her feet, not noticing the empty bucket beside her. Clumsily, she sent the bucket rolling about noisily on the concreted stable yard. The noise awoke Rex, the Alsatian guard dog. The dog pricked up its ears and set off to investigate the source of the din.

Rex made little growling noises in his throat and bared his large white fangs as he padded stealthily along. He stopped and sniffed at the air a few paces away from where the witch was hiding in the shadows. The hairs on his back stood up and he gave a savage snarl as he prepared to attack his prey.

Mrs Eastly acted quickly. Pointing her magic broomstick at the dog, she croaked:

*Magic broom, magic broom,*
*Save me from this beast of doom.*
*Change this hound into a dog of clay,*
*Hear my command broom and obey!*

Immediately the broom leapt out of the witch's hands and began to circle the dog. Poor Rex was bewildered. He grew frightened as the weird object circled around him, drawing closer, ever closer. He gave a tiny whimper as he was enveloped in a cloud of red smoke that came from the broomstick. When the smoke cleared away all that remained of Rex was a heavy clay statue.

34

Still trembling from the shock of her fall and her encounter with the Alsatian, Mrs Eastly peered around the yard to see if she could find where the ponies were stabled. Her task was easy. The stables were all in a line and each had the name of its occupant painted on it, together with the first name of the owner. "Thanks, girls," she muttered. "Even my dull-witted stepsons will be able to find what they are looking for." Then she thought of something that made her grin. She dragged the statue of Rex in front of the Ponyteers' stables. She patted its head and cackled, "There now, my nice little doggy. Take care and look after the ponies until my boys come round to collect them!"

The witch did not spend any more time loitering about the place. She flew back to Red House Farm without any mishap and had a nice hot bath before retiring for the night.

Lying in bed, she congratulated herself, "Clever girl," she said out aloud, "you've found out all that you wanted to know."

Unable to sleep, she sat up and drew a map of the riding school, sketching in the figure of the ornamental dog that she had left lying in front of the stables. She carefully marked the position of the Ponyteers' ponies and underlined their names in red! Satisfied now that the job was well done, she switched off her bedside light. But still she didn't sleep, she thought of something else and it worried her. It was the moon. That sliver of a moon was going to grow bigger every night. The brighter the moon the easier it would be for her stepsons to be detected, so the job had better be done quickly. She made up her mind to brief the boys first thing in the morning and she would be decisive. No ifs or buts, she would instruct them to steal the ponies as soon as it was dark that night.

Satisfied her plans would be carried out successfully, Mrs Eastly turned on her side and this time she did fall asleep and she dreamt contentedly about the misery that the theft of their ponies would bring to the Ponyteers.

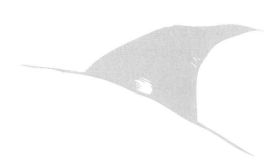

# CHAPTER SEVEN

## THE WITCH FORCES THE TWINS TO CARRY OUT HER PLANS

After breakfast next morning, Mrs Eastly began her briefing. With one sweep of her bony hands she made a space for her map on the kitchen table. "Study that carefully," she snapped. When she was absolutely sure they knew where the ponies were stabled she struck a match and burnt the map. "Always destroy incriminating evidence," she said. "You got that?" No reply from the boys, they didn't want to do the job she had asked them to do. It just wasn't right. Their consciences told them so. Bill and Andy were 16, going on 17 years old now and fed up with their stepmother and all her wicked ways. But they were scared of her magic broomstick.

"Take the big truck," she said, "Go round and round the village and the riding school today, and keep going until you are absolutely certain that you've got the layout of the place. You'll see there's a large padlock and chain on the main gate; make sure you take the heavy cutters to deal with that. Once inside, the rest should be easy. Do the break-in at three o'clock tomorrow morning, everybody will be asleep by then." She gave them a cold, challenging stare, "Do you find any problems with that?"

Bill and Andy shuffled their feet uneasily. Andy, who had seen the poster in the butcher's shop, spoke out bravely, "Why do we have to do this, Ma? Those girls only want to help people."

"You'll do it because I've told you to do it." The look on her face was menacing. Bill chimed in, "And I'm fed up with all this stealing. The house is full of stolen goods and one day the police will catch us, Ma, and we'll all end up in prison, and I don't very much fancy that. Come on, Ma, please, change your mind; it's a bad thing you're asking us to do. Just call the whole thing off."

Mrs Eastly was almost beside herself with rage. "Call the whole thing off! How dare you question me like that? Three o'clock in the morning you go in and steal those ponies. I expect you back with them at four o'clock at the very latest. Is that understood?"

The boys moved towards the door.

"Where do you two think you are going?" she demanded.

"We're going out. We want to talk things over," said Andy.

They had barely reached the centre of the farmyard when their stepmother appeared at the door, she was brandishing her broomstick. "Come back inside at once," she screamed, "Or do you want to see some magic?"

The boys hesitated for a moment before reluctantly returning to the house.

"Three o'clock in the morning," commanded Mrs Eastly.

The twins quickly nodded their heads, "Yes, Ma," they replied meekly. "Three o'clock in the morning."

Mrs Eastly showed her teeth in a sly grin. "Right then," she said, "I'll put this away – for now!" And she put the broomstick in a corner of the room where it stood against the wall, looking as harmless as any ordinary household broom.

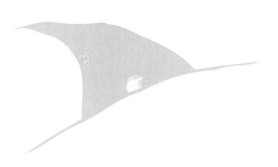

# CHAPTER EIGHT

## THIEVES IN THE NIGHT

On the same morning Witch Eastly was briefing her stepsons, the Ponyteers were returning to the stables after visiting the spot where Flikka had thrown Alison into the ditch. Flikka's hoof marks were still visible on the stretch of road where the fox had startled him. It was at Alison's request they had returned there, a journey she asked them to undertake several times more before her bad memories finally faded away.

They were passing the lane leading up to Red House Farm, when Lindsey, who could hear a pin drop at a hundred paces, said, "Listen, did you hear that?"

"What was it, Lindsey, what did you hear?"

"Thought I heard a woman screaming."

They all stopped to listen.

"Was it bad?" Alison asked.

"Awful. Our village choir wouldn't have her and they're desperate," said Lindsey.

The girls laughed, listened again but heard nothing. "Whatever it was, it's stopped now," said Leanne. "C'mon, I've lots to do at home. You lead the way, Alison?"

"Will do," said Alison, taking the lead.

Lindsey stayed at the riding school with Alison to help with the mucking out. Leanne went home to help her mother. They had all decided that tomorrow morning was early enough to talk about what they should do next.

Leanne and Lindsey woke up the following day to find the sun shining, and already it was pleasantly warm. "Warm enough to have breakfast in the garden," said their mum, bringing out milk, cereal and hot buttered toast and laying it on the patio table.

There was still some early morning mist about, particularly at the top of Tinsall Hill but gradually the sun dispersed the misty haze, making it clear enough for them to see the Sandstone Trail. Now, under the sun's full glare, the trail glowed like a rich golden ribbon that stretched across the full range of the hill.

Lindsey was putting marmalade on her last piece of toast when the doorbell rang. She heard the door being opened. Then came the sound of muffled voices and the sound of someone crying. Before Lindsey realized what was happening, Alison came running from the house into the garden. Her face was stained with tears.

"Alison, Alison, what's wrong, what's happened?" Leanne asked. The sisters were upset to see their friend looking so distraught and unhappy. They sat her down at the table, put their arms round her and did their best to comfort her. Alison, choked with emotion, was quite unable to speak. Alex felt upset and helpless; it distressed him to see her crying so pitifully.

At last Alison had recovered enough to try and tell them what had happened and in between sobs, said, "They must have come in the night. They came and took them away. All three of them – gone! Oh, Leanne, Lindsey, what are we going to do?" Alison seemed fraught with despair. Her body shook and she slumped down with her head on the table.

Leanne was the only one who had stayed calm. "Who came in the night, Alison? And what do you mean, all three of them have gone?"

"Our ponies, Leanne," sobbed Alison. "Poppy, Peace and Flikka. Someone came in the night and took all three of them away, and…and Rex, poor dog, he's disappeared too. They must have taken him as well. And you know what – they left a clay statue of him just to remind us. How cruel can that be?"

The news was so awful, even Leanne was stunned into silence. Lindsey began to cry with Alison.

Mrs Rawlins came out of the house with Leanne and Lindsey's mum. Mrs Rawlins said, "I have to go home now, Alison. The police will want to talk to your dad and me, to see if we can help with their enquiries. Sorry love, but we'll have to go…"

"No, Mum, please let me stay with Leanne and Lindsey, Mum – please?"

"What do you think, Julia?" asked Mrs Rawlins.

"Frankly, I think that she's better off here," said Mrs Farroll. "The girls will probably want to come to terms with the problem in their own way – just the three of them, together."

"I think you're right," said Mrs Rawlins, giving her daughter a farewell hug. "Better for my Alison to be with her friends at such a bad time as this."

Leanne looked around for Alex. He was missing. "Do you know where he is?" she asked Lindsey.

"He told me he was going to play football with his pal, Ginger Tomkins. I think he was upset when he saw Alison crying."

"At least he's out of harm's way, that's good, that's probably the very best thing for him. He's far too young to be involved in any of this. Bless the man who invented football," said Leanne, raising her eyes to the sky.

"Do you think the police will find out who did it?" Alison asked.

"'Spect they will," said Leanne. "But we can't just sit here and wait, can we? We have a motto, remember?"

"If you need any help, or you are afraid, call the three Ponyteers and they will come to your aid," chorused Alison and Lindsey, together.

"Our ponies will be frightened and afraid," said Leanne. "And if we're really serious about what we said, then we have to do something about it. Right?"

"Right," said Lindsey, with a determined look on her face. "I'm with you, Leanne."

"And you can count on me all the way," said Alison, looking equally determined, "but where do we go to look for them, where do we make a start? Have you any idea, Lindsey?"

Lindsey shook her head and said sadly, "Haven't a clue. Perhaps we should leave it to the police, after all?"

"No, we shouldn't," said Leanne, "We've got to live up to our motto and that's that. Listen you two, put on your thinking caps, you were at the stables most of yesterday afternoon, did you notice anything unusual – anything at all? That's the sort of question the police will be asking your parents, Alison."

"We-ll, there was one thing," said Alison, hesitantly, then she shook her head. "No, I don't think that could have had anything to do with it…"

"Never mind what you think," said Leanne, impatiently, "What was it you saw. You saw something, didn't you? Then tell us, Alison, what it was it that you saw?"

43

"That black truck. Lindsey saw it too, didn't you, Lindsey?"

"Oh, yes, that black truck," said Lindsey, with a new spark of interest. "The one that went round and round the village like it was lost, that's the one you mean, isn't it Alison?"

"Yes, that's the one."

"How do you mean, round and round the village?" said Leanne. "Did it pass by the riding school?"

"Yes, 'course it did," said Lindsey. "I told you, it was like it was lost. Kept slowing down at the riding school. I thought they were going to stop and ask us the way to somewhere, but they didn't."

"How many times did it pass by the riding stables?" asked Leanne.

"About four times, I think," said Lindsey.

"More like six, Lindsey," said Alison.

"And the driver, what did he look like?" said Leanne.

"Don't know. There were two in the cab but they were all muffled up so we couldn't see their faces."

Leanne was amazed and excited; she had struck gold with her very first question. "Listen," she said, "And think carefully. Was there a name on the side of the truck? Did you notice a name?"

"Yes, we did," said Lindsey. "And we remembered it because it was so funny. It made us laugh, didn't it, Alison?"

Alison smiled weakly but was still feeling far too upset to laugh.

"What was the name on the truck, Lindsey? What was the name?" Leanne could barely disguise the excitement in her voice.

"BEASTLY," replied Alison and Lindsey in unison. "That's why it's easy to remember, because it's such a beastly name."

44

"Brilliant," said Leanne, "You've done well, Alison and Lindsey. Now, wait here. I'm going to pop up to the house and check to see if the name Beastly is in the telephone book; if it is, then it will give their address. Won't be long, five minutes, okay? Wait 'til I get back." Alison and Lindsey waited and worried.

When Leanne returned, they could tell by her face that their luck was out. "Nothing under 'B' that even resembles Beastly," she told them flatly. "But don't worry," she added with some encouragement when she saw the two unhappy faces, "We've done pretty well so far, thanks to you, Alison and Lindsey."

"What else can we do?" Alison asked.

"Check the scene of the crime," said Leanne, imitating the voice of a detective they'd seen in a recent film. "That's our next step, okay? But first we'll go to the house and make a flask of tea and some sandwiches. We'll take them with us in case we get hungry. You know, you guys, I have a feeling that it may take the rest of the day before we solve this case." Leanne sounded so optimistic and so sure of their ability to "crack the case" that Lindsey and Alison managed to laugh at last.

"That's better," said Leanne, "And you'll laugh some more before the day's out, because we're going to get our ponies back and I promise you we'll get them back today!"

Half an hour later they had packed sandwiches and drinks into a rucksack and were outside the gates of the riding school. They saw that the riding school gates were swinging wide open. A broken chain and padlock were lying on the ground where the thieves had dropped them. The policeman standing at the gate recognised Alison. "Bad news this, Alison," he said. "But don't you worry, we've got a good idea who did it." Alison and Lindsey were so heartened to hear this that once again they were tempted to call off their own investigation and leave it all to the police. But Leanne would hear none of it, she was determined to get their ponies back themselves.

They asked the policeman if Rex the guard dog had returned. "No, there's only the statue." He scratched his chin and commented, "Funny business, that. Personally I think that whoever played a trick like that must be really sick."

Leanne left Lindsey and Alison with the policeman while she crossed the lane to inspect deposits of sand opposite the riding school gates. She called to her friends and asked them to come over and see the tyre patterns embedded in the sand. "They're like large letter 'V's, aren't they?" said Alison.

"That's exactly what I think. Do you think that they could have been made by that black truck?" asked Leanne.

"Can't think they could have been made by anything else," said Lindsey. "It must have been a heavy truck to make such deep grooves."

"Beastly," mused Leanne, "There's something odd about it. I mean, why isn't it in the phone book?"

Just at that moment a small van passed by with the name "I Slaughter, Family Butcher" painted on it. Ike was driving the van. He waved to the girls and they waved back

"That's it! That's it!" Leanne cried out, leaping into the air with excitement.

"What's it?" asked Alison, looking completely bewildered.

"I Slaughter," said Leanne. "It's the initial 'I' for Ike, correctly placed before the name 'Slaughter'. So, where's the initial that should be painted on that old black truck before the word beastly? It's missing – unless…" she paused. "Unless the first letter of Beastley is the missing initial, the one that we've been looking for?"

"So that would mean the correct name on the truck would be 'B Eastly," cried Lindsey.

"That's right," said Alison, "The truck was very dirty – remember, Lindsey – that's why we couldn't read the name properly?"

"There's one way to make sure," said Leanne, "Let's try the phone book again."

Lindsey ran like a hare to the house. She was the first to get there. By the time Leanne and Alison arrived she had already opened the phone book and was stabbing a finger at the name, "There it is," she shouted, triumphantly. 'B Eastly and Sons, Red House Farm, Brookdale, Near Tinsall'." Leanne and Alison peered over her shoulder to see for themselves. Then they all hugged and congratulated each other. Lindsey suggested, "Perhaps we should have started a detective agency?" And that set them off laughing until they remembered the seriousness of what they had to do.

They had no time now to stop for a picnic and ate their packed lunch as they hurried along the lanes – hot on the trail of their missing ponies!

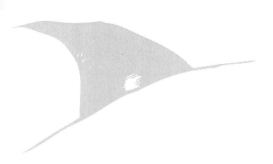

# CHAPTER NINE

## RED HOUSE FARM

As the girls left the road to take a short cut across the fields that led to Red House Farm, a narrow stream halted them in their tracks. When it rained, surface water usually drained down Tinsall Hill into the stream, making it flow quite swiftly, but it had been a hot dry summer and, denied water from the hill, the stream flowed sluggishly over an ever-thickening bed of mud. The girls studied it carefully and decided that it was too wide to jump, so they looked around to see if there was another way they could reach the opposite bank. They were lucky, not 20 paces away, Alison spotted a roughly made bridge constructed out of old railway sleepers and without hesitation, they crossed it. "Not much water, plenty mud!" commented Lindsey, after she had safely negotiated the stream.

They were now crossing a wheat field that had recently been harvested. The short stubble was tough and sharp and it crunched under their feet. "Ouch! Oh, my poor foot, should have put shoes on instead of sandals," exclaimed Alison. She was hopping about on one leg, rubbing a sore foot.

A few minutes later they climbed over the field's boundary gate and stood in a narrow country lane. "Which way, left or right?" Alison asked.

"Should be right, in fact there's the sign, see?" Leanne pointed to it.

The sign saying "Red House Farm" had been nailed to a broken, rotting post, which had fallen over and was partially blocking a long dirt road leading up to Red House Farm. The road was flanked on either side by a high hedge.

Alison and Lindsey had already taken a couple of steps up the road when Leanne called them back. "No, Alison, Lindsey," she said. "They're bound to see us if we take that road. We've got to get in and out of the farmyard with the ponies before they even know we've been there, otherwise we'll never make it."

"Creep up to the house on the other side of the hedge then. They won't see us from there," suggested Alison.

Leanne thought that was a good idea, so they kept the hedge between themselves and the road until they reached a point near to the farmhouse where there they stopped a minute to take a breather and decide what they should do next.

"Remember that day when Alison wanted us to take her back to the spot where she had been thrown by Flikka?" said Lindsey, who was enjoying her well-earned rest.

"What about it?" Leanne asked.

"I told you I heard a woman screaming. Well, this is the place the screaming came from, remember?"

"That's right, Lindsey, I listened when you told us, but I didn't hear anything," said Alison.

Leanne shivered, "Know something. I've got a really bad feeling about this place. Gives me the creeps. So, keep your heads down, you two. Don't break cover – and Linz – no noise, okay!"

"Okay."

Whilst they were resting and chatting away, Lindsey's curiosity got the better of her; she wanted to know what was at the other side of the high hedge. She peered through a gap, "Doesn't look like Red House Farm to me," she sniggered, "More like Patchwork Farm, I'd say." The others stopped talking and took a look for themselves. Alison giggled, she couldn't help it; Lindsey's description was spot on. Originally the house had been painted red, but now the paint was peeling off the outside walls and hanging down in strips. Some of these strips had fallen to the ground exposing large areas of red sandstone that, through dampness, were now turning distinctly black!

They were still whispering about the house when Alison interrupted and asked them to look at something that had caught her eye. She was pointing in the direction of Tinsall Hill.

"What do you want us to see?" Lindsey asked.

"There," said Alison. "Everything on Tinsall Hill is green and beautiful except for that area I'm pointing to. Why?"

No wonder Alison was curious. The sun was shining down on the hill and it bathed the trees, shrubs, grass and everything that grew on it in a rich golden light – except for one small area which looked completely barren. Leanne knew part of the answer, and told them as much as she knew. "The locals call it 'the dark side of the hill'. They think it was caused by a bomb that fell there during the war. That's over 60 years ago now. But nobody seems to know for sure. It's a mystery. But whatever happened, it left that part of the hill looking…"

"Dead!" Lindsey said.

"And you're dead right, Lindsey," said Alison. "Ugh! Just to look at it gives me the creeps. You won't find me going there – ever!"

After a while they had to stop speculating about the reason why nothing ever grew on the dark side of the hill, because Leanne told them that, however scared they felt, if they were to get to the house unobserved, they would have to approach it from the dark side of the hill. "All that dead and rotting undergrowth will give us good cover to crawl though," she said.

So they circled around until they were approaching the farmhouse from that direction and they crawled like snakes until they reached what had once been the perimeter fence of the farm. The fence was hardly recognisable as such, it had long since fallen down and now grass and weeds had taken over and grown up amongst the splintered woodwork. "Pooh!" Lindsey exclaimed. "Stinks, smells something rotten!"

"That's because it is rotten," said Alison and wriggling to get closer to Lindsey, she made the dry undergrowth rustle.

Leanne placed a warning finger to her lips, "Shush, you two," she said softly, and raising herself on her elbows she surveyed the farmhouse and farmyard, which was only a stone's throw away.

Not a sound came from the farmhouse. Leanne signalled for Lindsey and Alison to follow and, crouching low, they covered the ground between the boundary fence and the house in just a few seconds.

"Look! Can you see what I see?" Lindsey whispered.

Partly hidden by a jeep and the corner of a large shed they saw the black truck! A trail of sand ran up to its wheels and in the sand were the telltale "V" marks of the tyres, identical to the marks they had found opposite the stable gates. The Ponyteers, convinced they had traced their ponies, punched the air in silent jubilation.

"Flikka, Peace and Poppy can't be too far away," said Leanne, confidently. "Keep your eyes peeled, okay?"

They looked around. Between the boundary hedge and the farmhouse lay the farmyard; it must have been neglected for years and was badly potholed. In the centre of the yard stood a very large tank precariously supported at each corner by old building bricks. The bricks raised the tank about a metre above ground level.

Lindsey giggled nervously. "Hush, what's so funny?" Leanne whispered.

Lindsey pointed to a long clothesline, which stretched from one end of the farmyard to the other, "Plenty pegs, no washing," she laughed.

"Not so loud, Lindsey," warned Leanne, with her finger to her lips. "Look beyond the tank, near the hedge. What do you see?"

The girls saw a broken down shed-like building, half hidden by foliage from the thick boundary hedge. "That's where the ponies must be," said Leanne. "Come on, let's find out."

There was no cover for them between the farmhouse and the shed so they retreated to the safety of the weeds and long grass at the boundary fence. From there they crawled like snakes again until reaching the section of the high hedge that grew behind the shed. "Made it," said Leanne when they got there and they all sighed with relief. No one in the house had seen them!

The high dense hedge had offered them perfect cover. The Ponyteers congratulated themselves on being invisible.

"Peek-a-boo," sang Lindsey, peering at the house through a gap in the fence, "Peek-a-boo, I see you, but you can't see me."

"Nice one, Lindsey," said Alison, "But can you see the shed?"

"Right under my nose. Come and look for yourself," said Lindsey.

Both Alison and Leanne located the shed and Lindsey, with her sharp ears, said that she could hear something moving about inside it. Then Alison, her eyes glued to the peephole, said that through a crack in the shed wall she was sure that she could see something white moving around inside. She was convinced that it was Flikka.

"There's only one way to find out," said Leanne. "When we were crawling round I saw there was a window on the other side of the shed. I'll take a chance, I'll go round there and see what I can through the glass."

"But what if they catch you?" Lindsey asked anxiously.

"If they do, keep under cover of the hedge and return the way we came and go straight to the police, okay?"

Leanne noticed that her sister was trembling, "Don't worry, Linz, they've got to catch me first!" And having said that, she was gone.

She was back in next to no time, breathless with excitement. "They're in the shed alright, all three of them, and they look perfectly okay to me." Hidden from sight behind the hedge the girls hugged one another joyfully at hearing Leanne's good news.

"Okay," said Leanne when the hugging was over, "What we've done so far is the easy bit. Getting them out might be noisy. Maybe they'll hear us? If they do, they'll try to stop us. Chase after us. You both okay about that?" Alison and Lindsey nodded okay, but they were both feeling frightened now, almost ready to panic and run!

Before the Ponyteers could make another move, they heard a door opening and the sound of voices coming from the farmhouse. Then they could hear footsteps crossing the concrete yard. The voices were louder now. They were boys' voices and they seemed desperately unhappy. One of them began to speak and they could hear quite clearly what he said, "I'm sure Ma said that we were to boil them up for dog meat, there's enough dog meat here to keep all the dogs in Cheshire happy for over a year."

"I don't want to kill them," said the other, "but I'm frightened of that magic of hers. I can't take any more of that!"

"I know, I feel the same. What I'll do is light the fire under the tank. I refuse to do any more than that. If she wants them killed she can do it herself, what do you say, Bill?"

"Same as you, Andy. She can do what she likes to me, but I'm not going to kill those ponies."

Peering through the gap in the hedge, the terrified Ponyteers saw one of the boys strike a match and light the paper and sticks that were underneath the tank. Smoke was billowing up and into the air when Mrs Eastly looked through her kitchen window and saw what was happening. Her ugly face became contorted. Yelling and screaming she came running out of the house, "Fools, idiots, what do you think you are doing?" The twin boys shrank back from her, looking desperately afraid.

"We thought that was what you wanted, Ma. We thought you were going to boil them up for dog meat. We were only trying to help."

"If there's any thinking to be done, it'll be done by me, not you. Understand?"

"Yes, Ma," they replied, meekly.

"Right, I'll give you just ten seconds to put out that fire. Ten seconds! If it's not out by then you'll make me angry and you know what that means."

The twins leapt to do as they were told. They worked frantically, throwing bucket after bucket of water from the tank onto the flames while their stepmother harangued them. "Faster! Faster! Put it out! Put it out! Fools, idiots," she screamed, "That smoke can be seen for miles around, they'll think the whole of Delamere Forest is ablaze. Before you know it you'll have all the fire brigades and police in Cheshire swarming all over us. Go on, put it out! Put it out!"

The boys worked as hard as they could, each bucket full of water making a loud hissing noise as it fell onto the burning wood. Clouds of steam rose into the air.

Mrs Eastly supervised the boys' fire-quenching efforts. At a safe distance the Ponyteers took the opportunity to study her appearance. She was a large, heavy-looking woman with exceptionally long arms. A trailing black dress touched her toes, but its tight sleeves were too short and exposed thin, bony wrists and claw-like fingers. Dark, greasy hair streaked with grey hung down either side of her long, hooked nose. Surely that was the nose of a witch?

At last the fire was extinguished and with their faces glistening with sweat, the boys leaned against the water tank to rest.

Mrs Eastly hadn't stopped shouting at them all the time they were working, and now she was out of breath. But after gulping down one or two mouthfuls of fresh air she was able to shout again, "Go on, get into the kitchen," she ordered. "Go on, quickly, the two of you. I'll tell you how to get rid of those ponies, cash in hand and no mess. Yes, cash in hand and no mess, that's what we want." The twins meekly followed her into the house and the door banged shut.

"Isn't she a horrid woman, shouting at the boys like that?" Leanne said.

"They ought to make a tape recording of her shouting and then make her listen to it – 24 hours a day – that might cure her!" Alison said.

"Fat chance of that," said Lindsey.

"I know. I know. But forget about it for now," said Leanne. "Listen, I'm going to find out what she's up to. You heard her; she's going to tell those boys how to get rid of the ponies. Wait for me, I'll be back in a minute," and before they could find a single word to say in protest, Leanne had disappeared!

On the way to the house Leanne picked up the box she had used to stand on to see through the shed window. She placed it quietly on the ground outside the open kitchen window and stood on it at just the right height to hear but not to be seen. Old witch-face Eastly was talking, "Soon it will be Race Week in Doncaster…the St Leger, oldest horse race in the country…thousands turn out to watch it…Doncaster's the most important town in England during Leger week…"

"Is that where you want us to sell the ponies, Ma, is that what you want us to do?" Andy said, interrupting her.

Andy's stepmother turned her cold glinting eyes on him, "Sorry, Ma, didn't mean to interrupt, Ma."

"As I was saying before, thousands from all over the country will be flocking into Doncaster. There will be horse sales every day. Easy to get rid of the ponies there, and no questions asked. No problem."

One of the boys tried to ask her a question, but she cut him short. "I've written on this piece of paper what the bottom price is. If they offer you anything lower, don't accept it – just walk away. They're worth a lot more than the asking price, so you'll get plenty more chances. You'll sell them all right, but cash in hand, you hear? Cash in hand!"

"Okay, Ma – cash in hand – we won't forget."

Leanne had heard enough. She climbed down from the box, but instead of returning to Lindsey and Alison she decided to act on an idea that had just entered her head. If successful, it would give them just that bit of extra time they needed to make their escape.

Out of sight from the farmhouse windows, but within sight of the girls, she carried the box to one of the farmyard clothes posts and stood on it while she deftly untied the clothesline.

"What's she doing, Alison?" whispered Lindsey, unable to hide the fear in her voice.

"Dunno, we'll have to wait and see, won't we?"

They watched as Leanne proceeded to untie the rope from the second clothes post. As the rope slipped to the ground, Leanne picked it up, coiled it neatly over her arm and calmly walked with it right up to the farmhouse door.

"What does she think she's doing?" gasped Lindsey, "She's just asking to get caught." Under her breath she pleaded, "Oh, Leanne, Leanne, don't do that, get away while you can…"

"No, Lindsey, don't say that." Alison's voice was full of admiration, "Don't you see what she's doing, Lindsey, it's a great idea, just look what she's going to do with that rope."

But Lindsey said that she couldn't, she was terrified of seeing what might happen to her sister so she closed her eyes tightly and prayed for her safe return.

# CHAPTER TEN

## THE ESCAPE

"You can open your eyes now, Lindsey," said Alison, quietly.

Lindsey opened her eyes in time to see her sister dart across the farmyard and squeeze through the hedge. The next minute they were all hugging one another; it was great to have Leanne back.

Leanne was out of breath after completing her difficult task but she soon recovered and told them how she had tied one end of the rope to the front door of the house and the other end to the kitchen door at the side. She smiled, "Just imagine, old witch face will have to climb out through the kitchen window now, they can't get out of the house by the doors."

Imagining the antics of Mrs Eastly trying to climb through the kitchen window made Lindsey and Alison laugh out loud. But by holding their hands to their mouths, they managed to stifle the noise.

Leanne said, "Well, it gives us just that extra few minutes we need, doesn't it?" adding cheerfully, "Now come on, you Ponyteers, let's get out of here – it's time to rescue those ponies!"

Emboldened by Leanne's example, Lindsey and Alison felt brave enough to leave the cover of the thick hedge and they followed her to the front of the shed.

Lindsey tried the door handle – it was locked! "Oh no," she cried and she twisted and turned the handle again and again. But it was no use, the lock was too strong and Lindsey's hands grew sore through twisting and turning the handle. She tried her best not to panic and tried to be calm like her sister, but that didn't work and she felt that all her newfound bravery was slipping away.

She took her hands away from the door handle. "What shall we do now, Leanne?" she asked helplessly.

"It's all down to Alison's Flikka now," said Leanne. "Flikka's our only hope."

"What do you mean?" Alison looked puzzled.

"If Flikka hasn't forgotten how to use those strong back legs of his, we'll be out of here in next to no time. Go on, Alison, tell him to kick the door down and then we can all go home."

Alison began to talk to Flikka. Her voice, weak and faltering at first, grew stronger as she went on. The three ponies inside the shed recognised the sound of her voice and were getting excited. Alison continued to talk to Flikka. The ponies became more and more lively, they whinnied and snorted and ran about as best they could in the narrow confines of the shed. Alison recognised that now was the time to give Flikka his instructions. "Come on, Flikka," she called, "kick the door down so I can give you a great big kiss on your lovely nose. Come on, my lovely Flikka, get out of that horrid place. Kick the door down, Flikka, then we can all go home. Come on boy, kick! Kick! Kick!"

Things in the shed suddenly became quiet and a note of urgency crept into Alison's voice. She thought all her pleas to Flikka had failed, "Oh please," she pleaded, "please don't let me down, be a good boy, please Flikka kick the door down."

Suddenly the silence in the shed was shattered by a tremendous bang on the door. "Oh, good boy! Good boy, Flikka," the three girls yelled; they didn't care who heard them now; they could see the large crack that had appeared in the door caused by the impact of Flikka's hooves. There was another loud bang and then creaking and groaning, as the door swayed for a moment before it came crashing to the ground. Flikka whinnied in triumph; he came trotting out of the shed with his head held high. He nuzzled up to Alison, who was now crying with joy. She kissed him on the nose. "That's for being a good boy, Flikka."

Mrs Eastly heard the noise coming from the shed and her face appeared at the kitchen window. When she realized what was happening she shook her fist at the Ponyteers and screamed instructions to the twins, "Stop them! Stop them! They're trying to escape." The twins ran to the kitchen door, anxious to obey instantly, but the door wouldn't budge.

"Won't open, Ma, something's stopping it," Bill cried out, in a frightened voice. "Idiot, use the front door then," she screamed. This time Andy tried. He came back. "It's no use, Ma, that one's stuck as well." Mrs Eastly looked through the window and saw the Ponyteers galloping away.

"The window, the window," she yelled. "Open the window wider so we can all get through. Go on, Andy, you first, your brother will help me out while you fetch the jeep." Andy did as he was told and was back in no time at all with the jeep, but found that his stepmother had got herself stuck – she was half way in and half way out of the window.

Bertha Eastly was very heavy and it took both of the boys to lift her clear and help her into the jeep. Her face was contorted with fury. "Put your foot down," she yelled. "Drive as fast as you can." Andy put his foot down hard on the accelerator and the jeep leapt forward. "That's it, that's it, drive as fast as this and we'll soon catch them up and when we do I'll turn them into something really nasty."

But fortunately for the Ponyteers, in all the excitement, the witch had forgotten her magic broomstick, her spell book and her magic powder. She had left all of her magic behind, hidden in her secret den. And without any of these aids, Mrs Eastly was just about as dangerous as a fat old killer shark that had lost every one of its teeth!

By this time the girls had galloped half way down the long dirt road and were well on their way to safety. Leanne was in the lead with Alison and Lindsey close behind. No saddles, no reins, they clung for dear life to the manes of their ponies for fear they might fall off. Approaching the stubble field Leanne saw that the gate was set at the wrong angle for them to jump it safely. She dismounted and opened it so that her sister and Alison could get through without stopping. As soon as they were through, she closed the gate and urged Peace forward to catch up with them.

Leanne had thought that the closed gate would halt the jeep and give the Ponyteers just enough time to escape to safety on the other side of the stream. But that was wishful thinking on Leanne's part because when old witch face saw the closed gate she didn't hesitate. "Drive through it!" she yelled at the boys. "Go on, smash it down, or we'll all end up in prison." Not daring to disobey, the boys carried out her wishes and ploughed the jeep straight through it. What remained of the gate lay on the field in splinters.

Hearing the crashing of the gate, Leanne gave a

quick look over her shoulder and saw the witch was now standing up in the vehicle, steadying herself with one hand, threatening them with the other.

"Come on, Peace. Come on, Peace," Leanne urged, whispering softly into her pony's ear, "They're gaining on us." And it was true; the jeep was now close enough for Leanne to see Andy's white face at the wheel.

"Come on, Peace, come on," she urged, and Peace, with a toss of her head to show that she understood, found the strength to gallop faster.

Looking ahead Leanne saw that her sister and Alison were now on the other side of the stream. They were safe. She breathed a deep sigh of relief.

Both of them were waving and yelling at her, telling her to hurry. "Be quick, Leanne," they shouted. "Be quick, Leanne, she's just behind you, she's trying to reach out and grab you. Jump, Leanne. Jump, before it's too late!"

Peace was now rapidly approaching the stream and as she cleverly adjusted her stride in preparation for the jump, a charge of new energy surged into her legs and powered a truly magnificent take-off. Afterwards Leanne said that she would never, ever forget Peace's mighty leap. "It felt as if we were sailing through the air in slow motion and then at last we landed safely on the other side of the stream."

The occupants of the jeep were not quite so fortunate. Either they did not know about, or had forgotten the existence of the stream. Still standing upright, Bertha Eastly saw it and yelled, "Brakes! Brakes!" Andy did his best, but the warning came far too late. The jeep teetered on the edge of the stream – up and down it swayed, then gently it slid nose first into the muddy water down below.

The girls watched open-mouthed as three wretched

figures emerged from the mud, shivering and dripping brown slime.

"What was that you said, Lindsey?" asked Alison. "You know, before we crossed the stream that first time?"

Lindsey remembered and grinned, "Not much water – plenty mud!"

Alison pointed to the mud-splattered trio. "I didn't know grown-ups liked playing in mud, Lindsey, did you?"

Lindsey was feeling more like her old self again, and cupped her hands to her mouth, shouting to the Eastlys, "Monsters of the deep, do you come in peace and friendship?"

Threatened by their stepmother, the twin "monsters of the deep" responded by hurling handfulls of mud at the Ponyteers.

Lindsey shook her head and in a voice of mock solemnity called, "It would seem that they have not come in peace and friendship!"

But the witch had the last word. "If it takes me a life-time, I'll get you," she shrieked. "I'll have my revenge, so watch out!" And then she began to laugh, a laugh that sounded horrible and threatening until it was drowned out by the sound of wailing police sirens and the engines of cars, their blue lights flashing as they sped up the long dirt road that led to Red House Farm...

"Come on, Lindsey, Alison," said Leanne, wearily, "It's time we went home." As they drew near to the riding school she stopped, "There's something I want to apologise for."

"What's that?" said Lindsey and Alison together.

Leanne hung her head. "I want to say sorry to you both. You were both right and I was wrong, I made an awful mistake, getting you involved in all this."

"Wrong? A mistake, what are you talking about?"

chorused Alison and Lindsey, completely forgetting how terrified they had been at Red House Farm.

"We should have left it all to the police," said Leanne. "My fault. I'll never make the same mistake again."

Lindsey, who was on the verge of saying 'I told you so' held her tongue for once and both she and Alison told Leanne that there was nothing to forgive, they wouldn't have wanted the ponies rescued any other way.

But then Leanne noticed that the expression on Lindsey and Alison's faces had changed. They looked scared. "Are you two okay?" she asked.

There was a pause and then Lindsey finally found her tongue. "That old witch face, she was so angry, didn't you see? She said if it takes a lifetime she'd find us and put a spell on us. She definitely wants her revenge."

"Don't worry," reassured Leanne. "You saw the police cars. Mrs Eastly will be in prison for a long time to come. She won't bother you or Alison again. Once she's in prison, she'll forget all about us, you'll see."

But Alison and Lindsey were still not convinced; they thought that the threat of the angry witch was very real.

Locked in her prison cell, Bertha Eastly remembered them all vividly and she was determined to have her revenge. It helped her prison sentence to pass by more quickly when she thought about all the unpleasant things she would do to the Ponyteers when the day finally came for her release.

# PART TWO

## ROMAN TREASURE

# CHAPTER ONE

## LAURA BECOMES
## THE FOURTH PONYTEER

Within a few days after the police had taken away Mrs Eastly and her twin stepsons, the phone rang at the Farrolls. It was Mrs Stuart, who called to tell them that Laura was waiting at the cottage for the girls to come and see her and that she had a surprise in store for them. She wouldn't say what the surprise was. She said, "You'll just have to wait and see."

It was a warm, sunny afternoon and Laura was leaning against the garden gate waiting for the girls to arrive. The heat stored in the gate's woodwork seeped through her dress sleeves and into her arms, making her feel drowsy and she felt her eyelids beginning to droop. Then, through half closed eyes, she saw the girls approaching, three of them smiling and waving. Her eyes opened wide and she greeted them, "Hi girls, I'm Laura, am I glad to see you?"

The taller girl of the group answered first, "Hi, Laura, I'm Leanne. This is my sister, Lindsey, and this is our friend, Alison."

"Hi! Great to meet you all. Mind, I know a lot about you already. Gran showed me those newspaper cuttings about Alison's rescue from the ditch." She gave them a friendly smile. "What's it like to be famous? No, don't answer that, Gran's waiting inside for us with tea and cakes." She paused. "But before we go inside can I show you a surprise waiting for you at the back?" Laura led them to the rear of the newly extended cottage and pointed. "What do you think about that?"

The girls gasped with pleasure at what they saw; standing on the cobblestones outside the stable was the most beautiful pony they had ever seen. It stood there quite motionless.

"Like a golden statue," said Lindsey, with awe in her voice.

"Isn't she lovely?" said Laura, proudly. "What do you think I should call her?"

"Juno," said Leanne without hesitation "Like the Roman goddess, Juno, that's what I'd call her."

Laura was delighted. "That's what I've decided to call her, but for a different reason. Tell you about that later, first let me introduce you to Juno."

One by one, Laura introduced the girls to Juno and they patted and stroked her while she stood very still enjoying all the fuss.

"Wait 'til you meet Poppy and Peace and Flikka," whispered Alison in Juno's ear, "they'll want to make you their friend too." And Juno raised her head and whinnied as if to show that she was heartily looking forward to that.

Mrs Stuart called them into the house for tea. The girls were able to spend a few hours chatting and getting to know Laura better. When it was time to say goodbye Laura told them that later that afternoon she was expecting a phone call from Professor Klopstock in San Francisco. Leanne thought that sounded really intriguing and when she had thanked Mrs Stuart for their delicious tea she asked Laura if she would like to share in a picnic at their tree house next day. Laura said nothing would please her more.

Next morning, Leanne, Lindsey and Alison were sitting round the patio table in the garden when Laura arrived.

"Thought the meeting was in the tree house," Laura said, taking a spare seat at the table.

"Dad banned it," said Leanne, resignedly. "He said the platform's too weak and dangerous for big lolloping creatures like us to play around on it anymore. He told us that we'll have to hold our future meetings here, or in the house."

"Well, if there's an accommodation problem, I'm sure Gran would let us meet in the cottage," said Laura.

"The only problem here is Alex," said Lindsey, "Within five minutes of Dad putting a ban on us, he and his pal, Ginger Tomkins, had taken down our head quarters sign and replaced it with a sign of their own."

"Dad said it was strong enough for them to use it, so why complain?" said Leanne.

"It's the way they laughed when they took our sign down, that's what gets me," said Lindsey sharply. "They thought they were putting one over on us, I could tell." She noticed her sister staring at her and added rather defiantly, "Well, it's true, Leanne, you know what Alex's like."

"No, it's not true and you know it. Forget it, Lindsey, we've more important things to discuss than that."

By this time Laura was looking decidedly uncomfortable. "Sorry, have I arrived too early?" she asked.

"No, you haven't arrived too early. Take no notice of Lindsey; it's her way of having fun. She's just trying to

wind us up, that's all. This meeting concerns you, Laura."
She shot a warning glance at her sister. In response, Lindsey
smiled as innocently as a baby.

"Okay, I'm listening," said Laura.

Leanne began to explain to Laura how they had come
to call themselves The Three Ponyteers and the reason why
they wanted to help people.

"You did it because of Alison's accident and also because
of what happened to me in San Francisco, didn't you?"

"Well, yes, that's what started me off thinking about it in
the first place." said Alison.

There was admiration in Laura's voice when she replied,
"Well, if you ask me, I think you guys are fantastic. Just
wish I was part of the team, that's all."

"That's what we wanted to ask you, Laura. We wanted
to ask if you would like to be the fourth Ponyteer, but when
we talked it over again, we decided that it wouldn't be
fair."

Laura looked puzzled. "Why wouldn't it be fair?"

"'Cos it would be too dangerous for you, that's why,"
said Lindsey bluntly.

"Dangerous? Are you guys teasing me?" Laura laughed.
"C'mon, how can helping people be dangerous?"

It was left to Leanne to convince Laura that they were not
joking. She told Laura the whole story, how Ike Slaughter,
the village butcher, had tried to help them get their message
across by giving their poster prime position in his shop, and
how their ponies had been stolen almost before the paint on
their poster had dried.

Then she went on to describe how they had set about
investigating the theft and about the big black truck and
the "V" shaped prints the tyre treads had left in the sand.
Laura listened intently as Leanne explained to her how

they had tracked the thieves down to Red House Farm and how Alison had persuaded Flikka to kick down the door of the shed where the ponies were imprisoned.

Laura thought Leanne's description of the old witch landing face down in a thick bed of mud was really comical. But the smile disappeared from Laura's face when she learned how Mrs Eastly had shaken her fist at them and vowed revenge and said that she would seek them out wherever they were and cast a spell on them.

Lindsey was even more frightened than Leanne or Alison because she thought that Witch Eastly hated her the most because she laughed at her and called her a monster.

"So you see, Laura," said Leanne, when they came to the end of their story, "it wouldn't be fair if we asked you to become the fourth Ponyteer, now would it? After all, you've troubles enough without any more. And if you joined with us, you would be exposed to danger too, and goodness knows, you've had more than your fair share of that already…"

Laura interrupted, "Witch or no witch," she said, firmly, "I still want to be the fourth Ponyteer. So, c'mon, I want to help the people who need help every bit as much as you do. And it wouldn't be fair if you didn't ask me to be the fourth Ponyteer, it would be really unfair if you left me out."

Leanne, Lindsey and Alison gave in to Laura's plea. Laura became the fourth Ponyteer and together they joined hands and recited the Ponyteer motto.

Mrs Farroll heard them as she came out with a special cake she had made for the occasion. Three chocolate figures on ponies decorated the top of the cake and as if by magic, Mrs Farroll produced one more, which she added to the cake with a ceremonial flourish to represent Ponyteer number four!

The Ponyteers gave four rousing cheers!

When all the excitement had died down, Laura took a sip of tea from her cup and then laid it back in the saucer. Tapping her cup with her spoon she immediately gained their attention. "My turn to say something now," she said. "First, thanks to everybody for allowing me to become part of the team. And thanks to Leanne for telling me the story about how the Ponyteers began and what they want to achieve. I'll try to help on that. And another thing, if old witch face Eastly tries to hurt you, she'll have to get past me first, okay? Right, that's all I've got to say about that, but having listened to your story, now how about you listening to mine?" Laura looked around to see what they would say.

"Okay, we're listening," they chorused.

Laura started her story at the beginning. She told them that her parents had been working with a Professor Klopstock in San Francisco on a robot called Jupiter that had exploded, killing both her parents and injuring the professor. She found that so difficult to talk about she lapsed into silence for a while.

Leanne felt sorry for Laura and said, "You don't have to go on. You don't have to tell us about it, Laura. Not if it makes you unhappy."

But Laura insisted and gradually managed to tell them everything up to the point when, just before she returned to England with her grandparents, Professor Klopstock had given her a Roman treasure map as a present.

The words treasure map, generated so much excitement, Leanne, Lindsey and Alison didn't want to talk about anything else but the treasure map. "The treasure map, where is it? Is it real? Show us," they demanded.

Laura, her composure now recovered said, "I haven't

got it with me. Show you tomorrow morning at the Tea Pot Café. Eleven o'clock. My treat, well..." she laughed, "actually Granddad gave me the money. To celebrate, he said! He prophesied I'd be the fourth Ponyteer by the end of the day, and you know, girls, my Granddad – he's nearly always right."

Leanne, Lindsey and Alison could hardly wait for the next day. Their minds were buzzing with curiosity, trying to work out what Laura would have in store for them when they met at the Tea Pot Café.

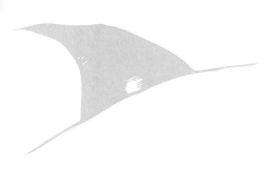

# CHAPTER TWO

## THE TREASURE MAP

The Ponyteers arrived at the Tea Pot Café at eleven o'clock in the morning, precisely. Almost too excited to speak, they tethered their ponies in the shade of a large oak tree close to a freshly topped up water trough.

Alison nudged Leanne and pointed to Flikka, happily flailing the air with his tail whilst enjoying a quiet nibble at the fresh grass with Peace. Nearby, Juno and Poppy were already behaving like old friends.

The four Ponyteers sat down at a table and waited for Mrs Potts to come and serve them.

Alison said quietly, "It'll be at least ten minutes before she gets around to us, those hikers were here earlier. She'll serve them first. Come on, Laura, don't keep us in suspense, have you brought the map?"

"Okay," said Laura. "Guess that's what I invited you to see." She pulled out a map from a large envelope and spread it across the table.

"Which way up is it?" asked Lindsey, who wasn't very good with maps.

"This way," said Laura, and the Ponyteers craned their necks, scrutinising it carefully.

"I took a good look at it earlier," said Laura. "See those two crosses, I think one of them marks where the Roman treasure is. Not sure about the other one though."

Leanne studied the map closely. "That cross is in the middle of some hatch marks Professor Klopstock's drawn on the map. D'you think he intended it to mark out a danger area, Laura? I think the area we are looking at is what the villagers call 'the dark side of the hill'."

"In that case it's strictly a no-go area," said Laura. "The professor is convinced that creatures of some kind or other are alive and living there, deep underneath that hill." Laura saw the incredulous looks on her friends' faces. "It's true, that's what he told me," she said. "And what's more he made me promise not to go anywhere near it until he comes to see me again. And when he does come, he promised that together we would solve the mystery of the dark side of the hill. I believe him; the professor always keeps his word."

"Did you say that creatures were living under the hill? Is that what you said, Laura?"

Lindsey was looking distinctly nervous.

"Yes, I did. And you mustn't go to try and find out. It's far too dangerous, Lindsey,"

"No danger of that, Laura. I'm not going anywhere near it," said Lindsey.

"Nor me," said Alison, I had a horrid dream about that place."

"Can you tell us about it?" asked Laura.

"Not much to tell, really," said Alison. "I dreamt I was looking for you three up on the dark side of the hill. You had disappeared; I thought you were in danger. I was worried. Then this little woman appeared. She had the smallest, darkest piercing eyes that I've ever seen. But she had a kind face and promised to show me where you were. So I followed her and she led me through an open door and along a passage that led deep down under the hill. I saw you in the distance just as a group of fierce-looking creatures came swarming down from some higher ground above. They were going to attack you and I called out a warning and we ran out into the open and back down the hill. They didn't follow us, but for a while we could hear their angry, muffled voices coming from deep down under the hill. I looked around to see if the door was still open but it had vanished and so had that kind little woman who had helped us. Then I woke up."

"Poor Alison, what a nightmare!" sympathised Laura.

Leanne was sympathetic too, but it didn't dampen her curiosity. "I'd love to find out more about those people, Laura, wouldn't you?"

"Yes, I am curious," replied Laura. "But the professor said it was a highly dangerous area and I gave him my promise not to go near it. So please, Leanne, won't you give the same promise to me?"

"Okay, Laura, I promise," said Leanne and she meant it.

The Ponyteers had no idea that everything that they had said had been overheard by the couple sitting at the table next to them. They were a Mr and Mrs W E R Crookes, who were property dealers in Chester. They really were a sad couple, totally bored with each other's company; they didn't say a word to one another unless it was about money. They found other people's conversation much more interesting than their own, so wherever they went, they indulged in eavesdropping. Today was no exception.

Mr Crookes had a cup of coffee raised to his lips when he heard Leanne mention Professor Klopstock's name. Instantly alert, he almost choked on his drink.

"What's wrong?" whispered his wife, more out of curiosity than concern.

"Klopstock," he whispered back to her. "We read about him in the paper about a year ago, remember? When it comes to making spaceships and rockets and robots, he's the man. The best. An amateur archaeologist as well."

"I thought he was dead. Killed when a robot exploded in America, in San Francisco."

"No, no. He was badly injured, but he wasn't killed. It was the little girl's parents who were killed." He nodded towards Laura. "That girl with the Yankee accent, I bet that she's their daughter."

"So why the interest?" his wife asked, still keeping her voice low.

"Because that's a map they're looking at. Klopstock was an archaeologist, lived in Chester for a long time after the war, didn't he? Put two and two together and what have you got? Roman treasure! I reckon that's a treasure map they're looking at and it's the genuine article, my dear." Mr Crookes was straining his eyes to try and see more detail on the map.

His wife said, "So what if you're right, there's nothing in it for us, is there?"

"I'm thinking about it," said Mr Crookes, patting down the few remaining hairs on his head before saying, "Our property business isn't paying us much of a return, is it?"

"You can say that again," was his wife's sneering reply.

He ignored her sneers. "If we could lay our hands on some of that treasure, our troubles would be over."

"Why don't you face up to it?" his wife said. "As a business man you're a failure. You tried to buy Red House Farm and it flopped. That woman, Eastly, ran rings round you. Made you look a real idiot."

"Sneer all you like," hissed Mr Crookes, "but you wouldn't refuse a share of the treasure if it were offered, now would you?"

Mrs Crookes didn't reply. What her husband had said was true. She would not refuse such an offer. The possibility of finding treasure dominated her mind to such an extent that it became full of greedy thoughts about golden rings and precious stones. She speculated about it for a long time and the tea in her cup went cold.

Mrs Potts came along to serve the Ponyteers with their drinks, homemade cakes and scones with jam and fresh cream. Laura insisted that the map was put away whilst they were eating, in case they made it sticky!

"What shall we do now then?" asked Alison, speaking with her mouth full of cream cake.

"Well, there's one thing," said Lindsey, "We can't take the ponies, and that's for sure. The treasure cave's on the Sandstone Trail and that's too narrow and dangerous for them."

Alison swallowed. "You're right, Lindsey. We'll have to go on foot. I don't know what everybody else thinks, but after seeing that treasure map, I just can't wait to get started."

The others felt the same way, and they all agreed to meet at Leanne and Lindsey's house early next morning.

"Better wear shoes, not sandals this time, Alison," Leanne said.

After Laura had settled the bill with Mrs Potts, the four girls mounted their ponies and made tracks for home. They were unaware that a small grey car was trailing them. Mr Crookes drove slowly, keeping a safe distance behind the small group of riders.

After they had stabled their ponies, Crookes followed even more cautiously, whilst his wife noted carefully where every one of them lived.

"They're going for it tomorrow morning. I heard them at the café. We'll follow and they'll lead us to it. By tomorrow night, we'll be rich!"

"What if they tell the police about us, after we steal the treasure from them?" asked Mrs Crookes.

"They won't be alive to tell the tale, will they?" He drew a finger across his throat. "Are you sure you're really in on it?"

His wife nodded. "I don't care what you do to those children as long as we get the treasure." Her face was set hard as stone.

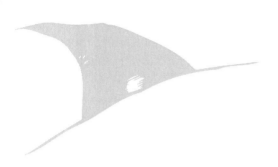

# CHAPTER THREE

## THE SECRET CAVE

Leanne and Lindsey hardly slept a wink that night. When they got out of bed the next morning their eyes were red rimmed through lack of sleep, but after a shower and breakfast they felt much better. The grandfather clock in the hall struck eight and eager to be off on the treasure trail, the girls took turns to look through the window for Alison and Laura. In between visits to the window they checked the contents of their rucksacks to make sure that as well as drinks and sandwiches, they had each packed a torch.

Lindsey raised her eyebrows when she saw Leanne return from a visit to the garage with a coil of rope. "What's that for?" she asked.

"In case we have to climb down into a cave, or whatever. You never know what may happen."

Alex sensed something was going on. All that whispering that was taking place between his sisters was a dead giveaway. He was being excluded. Oh yes! They were planning something big and they didn't want to let him in on it. But Alex was determined not to let them get away without him. He was washed, dressed and breakfasted as quickly as his sisters, and ready to go just as soon as they were. But he couldn't hide his curiosity. "What's happening? Where are you going?" he asked, as nonchalantly as he could.

"None of your business," snapped Lindsey. "You can't come with us, and that's that."

"Huh! That's what you think," Alex muttered and he took himself off and phoned his chum, Ginger Tomkins. "Hi, Ginger, got something to tell you…"

Alex spoke quietly, casting frequent glances in the direction of his sisters to make sure they couldn't hear or understand a word of what he was saying.

Lindsey suspected her brother was plotting to do something with Ginger and she tried her best to catch the drift of his conversation, but Alex kept his voice low and she couldn't make sense of what he was saying.

After he had finished with the phone, Alex disappeared into his room where his sisters heard him opening and closing drawers. "What's he up to?" said Lindsey.

"Just leave him, Lindsey," said Leanne. "Leave him to do whatever he has arranged to do with Ginger. They're too young to come with us – the climbing could be difficult for them – even dangerous!"

Alison and Laura arrived and half an hour later the four girls were on the Sandstone Trail, high up on Tinsall Hill. They were lucky with the weather, there were a few clouds in the sky but the forecast was generally good, warm and dry.

Looking down from the top of the hill, Laura could see where she lived and the riding school close by, but after they had walked a good way up the trail, none of the views were familiar to her.

"I think it's best if you take the map, Leanne," she said, "'cos you know this area better than me."

They walked on for about another half-mile before Leanne stopped and took a look at the map. She said, "Keep your eyes peeled for the letters JK. They're carved on one of those sandstone rocks that are scattered along the trail on the left. According to the map we can't be far away. And those initials should be easy to spot, says here they're at eye level."

Leanne passed the map round so they could all see exactly where they were in relation to trees, shrubs and rock formations that lined the left-hand side of the route. Then they walked slowly, scrutinising each rock for the special initials JK.

Laura was the first to spot what they were looking for. "Here they are," she cried, "but the initials are higher up on the rocks than you said."

They quickly checked with the map. Laura was quite right; the initials were higher than indicated on the map.

"Perhaps we've stopped at the wrong place," said Alison.

"No, this is the right spot," said Laura. "The initials JK are enough for me. A lot of people have walked on the Sandstone Trail since the professor carved his initials on that rock. All that walking must have worn the path down some, I guess."

Everyone accepted Laura's explanation and decided to try and look over the top of the rocks to see if the cave was there. Alison and Leanne were the tallest; they stood on their tiptoes, but it was hopeless – the sandstone barrier was far too high for that.

"Let me have another look at the map," said Laura. "On the other side of these rocks – about 20 paces in – the map shows another block of sandstone. And guess what?" She let out a shriek of excitement. "It should be the treasure cave! See, it's marked clearly on the map."

They clustered around her eagerly, wanting to see it for themselves. Laura was right, the professor's mark was on the map, they'd found it – they'd found the treasure cave! But Lindsey advised caution. She said, "We've got to see for ourselves that the cave is really there. That mark on the map doesn't prove anything."

"Lindsey's right," said Leanne, "We've got to check it out first, make sure it exists before we get too excited. Can you climb up on my shoulders, Laura? Should be high enough for you to take a peek over the top."

Within seconds Laura was peering over the top of the sandstone ridge. "It's there, alright," she called out triumphantly. "That large rock's there. It's got to be the entrance to the cave. It must be!"

Leanne was feeling the weight of Laura on her shoulders. "You're a bit heavy, Laura. Do you think you could get up on the top without any help, if I manage to keep steady?"

"Sure, no sweat, Leanne," said Laura, and using the cracks between the rocks like a ladder she reached the top of the ridge within seconds and was looking down at them.

"Anyone want a pull up?" she offered.

Leanne threw the rope to Laura. "No need to pull anybody up, Laura, tie one end of this rope to the tree beside you and then throw the other end down to me Then, we can all shin up – no problem."

Five minutes later they were standing beside the red sandstone rock that they calculated was exactly in the spot marked "Roman treasure cave" on the map.

Lindsey said, "But the million dollar question is, how do we get in? Where's the entrance? I can't see any. Doesn't look like a cave to me. For all we know, it could be just another rock like all the others."

It was true. Lindsey's comment made her sister and Alison, look glum.

Laura said, "Sorry, it's my fault. I should have read the professor's journal more thoroughly. I promised him I would but I didn't, I just skipped through it, mostly."

"But deep down you must know if there is a cave here, otherwise you wouldn't have brought us all this way, now would you?" said Leanne.

They all watched the strain on Laura's face as she put her memory to work. At last she came up with something. "It's true about the rock. The rock's right. The journal said something about a small hole in it, just large enough to take a hand. It said what it was for, but I can't remember, I can't…" Laura's voice trailed off miserably.

Alison didn't waste any time. As quick as a flash she was off to examine every inch of the rock to try and find a hole just large enough to take her hand. And she found it. She put her hand inside. "I can feel a wheel-shaped thing," she called out in a loud voice. "Don't know what it is. Come; see what you make of it, Laura. Perhaps it will remind you of what the journal said we had to do next?"

Laura groped inside the hole until she found the wheel. "It's a ratchet wheel," she cried. "I remember, I remember… Take care, everybody, I'm turning it, soon you'll see the door opening then we can get into the cave. Stand back, everybody."

Laura felt the wheel move under the pressure from her hand. "It's turning, It's working. Anything happening?"

"Yes! Yes. Keep turning it, Laura. A slab of sandstone at the front – it's sliding downwards – the entrance to the cave's opening!"

Laura turned the wheel until it stuck fast. "I can't move

it any more," she said. She took her hand out of the hole and wiped some sweat from her brow.

"Don't worry, Laura, the gap's opened wide enough for us to crawl through. Come on, Laura. Come round to the front and see it for yourself."

Laura joined the other girls. Kneeling down, she shone her torch into the space below. "The drop's about three feet from here to the floor of the cave," she said. "It will be an easy jump."

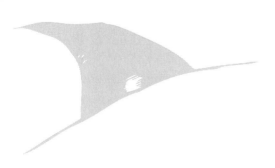

# CHAPTER FOUR

## TREASURE

"Who's going in first?" Lindsey asked. She was curious, she wanted to know what was in the cave, but she was nervous. Leanne proposed that Laura should decide who went in first, reminding everybody that it was Laura who had found a way into the cave.

"I will go in first, if you don't mind," said Laura, "I think the professor would expect me to. So I'll jump now, okay?"

They all agreed, and one by one they jumped down after Laura.

Once inside, they quickly switched on their torches to have a good look around. The cave was much larger than expected. It seemed to be oblong in shape, roughly four metres long, by three metres wide and almost two metres in height so that the roof cleared their heads easily.

Alison was swinging her torch about when the beam settled on something that almost made her jump out of her skin. At the far end of the cave she saw two Roman soldiers, with swords in their hands. They looked so life-like and as if they were standing on guard. Alison couldn't speak, she couldn't call out, and for a second she felt that she couldn't even breathe! Then the truth dawned on her; they weren't real Roman soldiers – they were robots! But what were they guarding? There didn't seem to be anything there for them to guard. She asked Laura if she knew about them.

Laura focused the beam of her torch on them and remembered that there was a warning about those robots in the professor's journal. "But I've forgotten what the warning was about. My fault – again!" She looked worried and called out in a loud voice, "Keep an eye on those robots, everybody. They're bad guys and that means trouble."

A call from Lindsey suddenly diverted them, "Wow! Will you take a look at this?" Her torch was shining on a row of golden ingots neatly arranged on a stone slab. "It's gold! It's gold!" she cried. "I'm sure it's gold and look, see all this other stuff – gold cups, gold plates – gold everything!" She held up a large golden cup for everyone to see.

"But come over here. Wait 'til you've seen this." The call came from Leanne and they all swung their torches in her direction. She held open the lid of a large wooden chest, which was filled to the top with gold coins. Scooping up a handful, Leanne let them trickle slowly through her fingers, the coins shone and glittered as they fell back into the box. "Wow! – It's raining gold," whispered Laura.

They were all still buzzing with excitement at what they had discovered when they heard a commotion coming from the direction of the cave entrance. Excitement was instantly replaced by fear. Who could it be? What could it be?

"Quick! Hide behind this chest," said Leanne. "I'll keep the lid up, give us more cover." In a flash the four girls were hidden behind the chest of gold coins. Huddled together, they switched off their torches, and kept as quiet as mice.

They heard a scraping noise followed by two distinct

bumps on the floor of the cave directly underneath the entrance. Then they heard high-pitched voices, complaining boys' voices.

"I landed on my bum and it's sore."

There came the sound of a laugh. "Mine's more sore than yours. Bet you it is."

The girls switched on their torches. There, in a pool of light, hands shading eyes, stood Alex and Ginger.

"What are you two doing here?" scolded Lindsey. But she was only pretending to be angry. Inwardly, she was relieved to see that her brother had come to no harm.

Alex finished dusting the sand from the seat of his trousers. "We followed you, tracked you down like Indians in the Everglades."

"The Everglades? They're all wet and swampy. It's dry and sandy here," said Lindsey, reminding him.

"I know that. Ginger knows that. But we were pretending we were in the Everglades – see?"

"And we would have got here sooner, but we couldn't climb over that high rock," said Ginger.

"So, how did you get here then?" asked Laura.

"Found an easier place to climb, further back, didn't we?" Ginger looked at Alex as much as to say, "Don't girls ask daft questions?"

It was then that Alex spotted the robots. Before anyone could stop him he ran towards them, shouting to Ginger, "Hey Ginger, come and see these swords." Ginger dashed forward, but Alex had a start and got to them first. He stood on a flagstone that separated the two robots and as he reached up to touch their swords, the ground beneath his feet seemed to give way slightly and then jolted to a sudden stop. The jerky movement almost threw him off balance. Recovering, he noticed a slab of rock in front of him slide upwards and peering through the widening gap, he could see more treasure stacked in a secret chamber that lay beyond the sliding door.

Then Leanne let out a scream of terror. The robots were moving. They had sprung into life! Both had their sword arms raised and were poised ready to make a downward strike. She leapt forward, managing to pull Alex clear before the robot's sword could complete its deadly downward swing.

Once Alex's weight had been removed from the flagstone, the sliding door abruptly closed and the robots' swords stopped in mid-air.

Leanne held Alex tightly in her arms and rocked him like a baby. "That's why we didn't want you and Ginger to come with us, Alex. We were only thinking about your safety."

Ginger was standing close to them for reassurance, "If Leanne hadn't pulled you clear, that robot would have chopped you clean in two."

But Alex, now secure in Leanne's arms, said boldly, "I was just about to jump when she did it!"

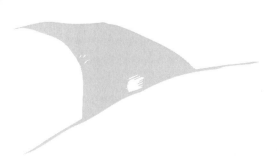

# CHAPTER FIVE

## PRISONERS

"Stop cuddling me, Leanne," complained Alex. "Ginger will think I'm a baby."

No sooner had Leanne released Alex than the sound of raised voices could be heard coming from outside the cave. Once again they all retreated to the large chest and cowered behind it. Switching off their torches they watched and waited.

Looking up towards the bright daylight of the entrance they saw the black silhouettes of a man and a woman. The two figures crawled clumsily through the opening and then scrambled down onto the soft sand of the cave floor. It was the same couple that had spied on them at the Tea Pot Café – the murderous Mr and Mrs Crookes!

The Crookes swept every cranny of the cave with their powerful torches and the children waited with baited breath as the beams came closer and closer, until finally the brilliant light settled on them, making them blink.

"I can see you," Mr Crookes called out in a voice that was harsh and cruel.

He waved a heavy walking stick at them and snarled, "Look, I want no bother from you kids. Come out from behind that box and get into that corner over there, where I can keep my eye on you. And be quick about it. Come on. Move!"

The children were too paralysed with fear to move, none of them could believe what was happening. Crookes yelled at them again, "Come on there, move – I'll give you to the count of three." He started to count and waved his stick about wildly. His stick struck the roof of the cave, which brought down a shower of sand that fell on the children's heads. The girls thought that the roof was collapsing and propelled Ginger and Alex into a far corner in the cave, which seemed to offer more safety. They all crouched there like scared rabbits.

Ginger Tomkins began to snivel and Leanne found Alex clinging to her arm. His fingers pressed hard into her and hurt. Leanne didn't complain or try to remove his hand. She bore the pain, anything to help Alex feel less frightened.

Crookes pulled out a black plastic bin liner from his inside pocket and instructed his wife to fill it with treasure. He was unaware that as he pulled out the sack, his wallet came out with it. It fell on the sandy floor close to his feet. At that moment another shower of sand fell from the roof covering the wallet completely.

Crookes grabbed the black sack from the hands of his wife. Greed had made her fill the sack so full it would impossible to carry it out of the cave without spilling some of the contents. Crookes discarded the top items of treasure and left them lying on the floor. Knotting the plastic sack he slung it over his shoulder, ready to leave. Looking down he saw that his wife had sunk to her knees, she was moaning and stroking the precious objects that he had discarded. Eyeing her with disgust, he demanded she get to her feet and ordered her out of the cave.

Mrs Crookes climbed awkwardly up to the entrance and slid outside. Mr Crookes hurled the sack of treasure up and out to her through the cave opening, then, unable to resist the urge, he turned back to gloat over his prisoners.

"I want you to take a look at me, you kids," he said, sarcastically, "You're looking at a man who can now afford a happy future. There's enough treasure in that bag to buy me anything I want and you are the kids who gave it me. I suppose I should say thanks, but I won't." He looked at them cowering miserably in the corner, but there wasn't a trace of compassion on his face. He shook his head and crowed, "Yesterday I was poor – bankrupt! Now, today, I'm rich! Take a good look at the man with the golden future." He paused and laughed. "Golden future, do you get it? And what's the future got in store for you, may I ask? Nothing! That's what the future has in store for you, nothing! And why?" he sneered. "I'll tell you why. It's because you are going to stay in this cave forever. Yes, you'll stay here and rot! And don't think that anyone will come and find you. Oh dear, no. No one knows where this cave is, 'cept you and me and I haven't told anybody, so nobody knows where you are. Nobody! But if it's any consolation, I may come back in a year or two's time to pick up a bit more treasure. Might even say hello to your skeletons. How's that grab you for a laugh?"

Crookes felt that he had gloated enough. Satisfied, he waved a mocking goodbye and left them. They heard him winding up the sandstone door. It closed with a clunk and now, without any light at all, the cave became as black as night again! Alex and Ginger began to cry, Leanne

94

and Lindsey did their best to console them and everyone switched on their torches.

"Why don't we just use one torch at a time – save batteries?" suggested Laura.

"Great idea! If you keep your torch on, Laura, we'll switch ours off," Leanne said.

"Do you think we'll ever find a way out of here?" said Alison, trying hard to keep her composure.

" 'Course we will," said Laura, sounding much more confident than she felt. "We'll find a way, just see if we don't."

Leanne was deep in thought. After a while she said, "Those robots are operated by springs." In the shadows of the cave the others nodded their agreement.

"So, if we load a few rucksacks on the spot where Alex stood, with that weight we should get the same reaction, okay?"

Everybody nodded again.

"Once we set the robots off swinging their arms, the springs are bound to run down – well, sometime, aren't they? And when they do run down and those swords stop swinging, we'll be able get into the secret chamber. Perhaps we may be able to find another way out from there?"

"Great thinking, Leanne," said Laura. "Hey, you guys, you heard that? Come on, let's do it!"

Leanne's idea and Laura's enthusiasm raised their spirits. Instead of having horrifying visions of being imprisoned forever, they were trying to figure out just how long it would take for those robot springs to run down, confident that once they got passed them and into the secret chamber they would find another way out.

The rucksack idea was a great success. The combined weight of Alison and Lindsey's rucksacks depressed the flagstone. It started to open the secret door to the chamber beyond and it set the robots' arms swinging, as one sword went up, the other came down. They waited for the mechanism to run down.

Whilst waiting, they considered an idea of Laura's. She thought that if they emptied two treasure chests that were lining the wall of the cave and piled them one on top of the other they would be able to reach the sandstone door. "The professor told me that sandstone was very soft…"

Alison interrupted, "What's that got to do with it? When we get there, the door's far too heavy for us to open and we can't get at the ratchet wheel either, 'cos it's on the outside."

Laura ignored the interruption. "As the professor said, sandstone is very soft, Alison. If we had a knife we could chisel our way through – eventually. And it will give us something to do while we wait for those springs on the robots to run down. Thing is, has anybody got a knife?"

First Ginger and then Alex produced a pocket-knife. They handed them to Laura, who tested the blades with her thumb. Both blades were strong and sharp.

"Thanks, boys," Laura said. "They're just the job, now we can get started."

Everybody helped to empty the chests and they gasped at the precious artefacts left strewn on the floor; jewellery of all descriptions, gold plate, there seemed no end to it. At last the job was finished and the chests were piled one on top of the other. The height was exactly right for them to start straight away with the chiselling.

Before climbing on top of the chests, Laura looked over to the robots. They were still swinging away with their swords. It looked as if they could go on forever!

Meantime Alison was first off the mark. She had climbed

on top of the chests and from the pinnacle she shouted, "Hey, you lot down there, ever seen a monkey use a chisel? No? Well, wait and see this." And she began to hack away at the sandstone door, singing whilst she worked, "Hey ho! Hey ho! It's off to work we go."

And everybody laughed, "Go! Go! Alison," they yelled.

Encouraged, Alison worked harder until she was shrouded in dust and then the dust came drifting downwards, settling on the children and turning them all quite red.

"It's working, it's working," cried Alison. "The sandstone's soft, like Laura said. We'll get out of here all right. It'll just take time, that's all."

It was Leanne's turn next. As they changed places, Alison said, "It'll take a good five hours to break through, that's my guess. And it depends on whether the knives stay sharp enough." She handed her pocket-knife to Leanne. Half of it had been worn away already!

Before Leanne started to chisel, they heard the sound of the ratchet wheel turning. Frightened, she half slid, half fell from the top of the chests onto the sandy floor. Alison and Laura dragged her into a shadowy corner of the cave. They all clung together expecting the evil Mr Crookes to reappear.

"'Spect he's come back for his wallet," whispered Alex.

"What wallet?"

Alex produced the wallet from his pocket. "I picked it up after he'd left. I was going to give it to you, Leanne. But the robots started to work again and I forgot."

"Hide it again, Alex, and be quick about it."

Alex hid the wallet under another pile of sand.

"I'm going to switch off my torch 'til we find out who's

out there. Is that okay with you guys?" Laura whispered.

"Okay, Laura," they whispered back. Once again they were in total darkness – waiting and shivering with fear.

# CHAPTER SIX

## THE RESCUE

The ratchet wheel stopped turning and the sandstone door to the cave opened. Six pairs of frightened eyes peered through the dim light to see if the dreaded Crookes had come back. First they heard a squeaking noise and then they saw what appeared to be a pair of shiny metal legs dangling over the edge of the cave entrance. It wasn't Crookes who was coming back; these legs belonged to a robot! The robot shone a torch and eased itself through the gap. Then, with a little push forward, down it came to make a perfect landing on its two mechanical feet. The robot flexed its joints, testing to see that all parts were still in good working order.

Laura shrieked with delight, "Juno! Juno! Juno! Is it really you?" She ran forward to meet her friend; Juno picked her up and twirled her around before setting her down, very gently. "So, you re-member Miss Sq-ueaky Legs then d-ear Lau-ra?" Juno's voice sounded as chopped up as ever and the light in her head winked and blinked rapidly, a sure sign that she was excited.

Laura's relief and happiness was plain for all to see. "Oh, my dear Juno, we've so much to talk about. But right now you've got to help us get out of here. A nasty man with an even nastier wife locked us in this cave and then left us here to die…"

"And this is the nasty man's name." Alex had popped up like a Jack-in-a-box to present Juno with WER Crookes' visiting card.

"Hey m-an, th-at's coo-l," said Juno. "T-ell me, what's y-our n-ame?"

"I'm Alex and this is my friend, Ginger Tomkins."

"Hi A-lex. Hi G-inger. I th-ink you are b-oth v-ery brave b-oys."

Alex and Ginger looked at the robot with something akin to hero worship in their eyes.

Juno studied the card that Alex had presented to her. "Th-ink I'll p-ay this guy a-nd his w-ife a visit this evening. You and me, A-lex, we'll h-ave a g-ood talk later, okay?"

"Sure, Juno. Hey, cool man. We'll talk about it later, sure thing, Juno."

Lindsey raised her eyebrows in amazement, saying, "I can't believe what I'm hearing, Alex thinks he's talking like an American."

It was then that Juno noticed the two Roman soldier robots; their swords were still swishing up and down in a lethal rhythm.

Juno said, "Hey, L-aura, I don't th-ink that you read the pro-fessor's journal thoroughly, d-id you?" Somehow the robot managed to convey a sense of gentle reproof through her flat stilted speech. She squeaked across to one of the robots and lifted up a small segment of armour on its back, a tiny click, and instantly the robot became as harmless as a statue. "On-off sw-itches," said Juno.

Laura blushed with embarrassment as she turned off

the switch belonging to the other robot. "I'll always read instructions thoroughly in future," she said.

Lindsey and Alison's rucksacks were still weighing down the flagstone between the Roman robots and the door to the secret chamber remained open. "Can we go in and have a good look around?" said Lindsey. She was almost bursting with curiosity to find out what was in there.

"Don't s-ee why n-ot," said Juno. "Go ahead. B-ut you'll f-ind it's j-ust the same as this one, ex-cept it has m-ore treasure. Th-at's why the Roman soldiers w-ere put th-ere. But there's no way out f-rom there. Th-ere's only one w-ay in and one w-ay out of th-is place, and by n-ow you all know where th-at is."

The amount of treasure they had discovered in the first chamber was huge, but they were quite overwhelmed by what they found in the secret chamber: gold and silver plaques, precious stones, bracelets of gold and silver, amber beads and figures carved out of ivory, not to mention the many large leather bags full of golden coins. Leanne had opened one of the bags and was fingering the coins. "Must be soldiers' pay, ready for when they returned from Rome," she said.

"But they never did come back, did they?" said Alison. She looked thoughtful. "If the Romans had returned, I wonder what this country would have been like today?"

"Well, we wouldn't have been speaking English, that's for sure," speculated Lindsey.

Alex and Ginger were examining some of the coloured beads. Their heads were close together and they were whispering excitedly to one another. They agreed that these beads were the best marbles they had ever seen, so they each took a pocketful to play with later.

"You must have caused a bit of a stir in the village when the locals saw you coming here," said Leanne to Juno.

"Th-ey didn't see me. I d-id this," said Juno. She slid back a tiny cover on her left arm and pressed a button that lay beneath it. For a second the robot appeared in a shimmering light and then there was – nothing. Juno had vanished completely!

A couple of seconds later, Juno miraculously reappeared. "Th-at's why th-ey didn't notice," she said. "They couldn't s-ee me. It's one of my latest im-provements. Do you l-ike it?"

The girls nodded an enthusiastic "yes" but secretly they had reservations and even Laura thought that invisibility would take a little time to get used to.

"I'm hungry," complained Alex. He moved towards the door of the cave with Ginger. Both boys were carrying their rucksacks; all they wanted to do now was to go home. The others were also ready; they felt physically and mentally drained. Without saying a word, Alison and Lindsey collected their rucksacks from the flagstone and the door to the secret chamber slid shut.

Leanne and Laura collected their belongings too, and they all helped each other to climb out of the cave.

Outside, Juno operated the ratchet wheel and as Laura and her friends turned towards home, they heard the heavy clunk that told them that the sandstone door to the Roman treasure cave had finally been closed.

Juno turned on her invisibility device as they neared the village. A group of villagers shook their heads in amazement when they heard and saw four girls and two young boys talking to someone who obviously wasn't there. "Kids these days," they muttered, "they just get crazier and crazier!"

Close to home, Leanne asked Laura what she thought they should do about the treasure. Without hesitation Laura replied that it should go to the museum. She said that she would phone and tell the curator about the treasure straight after breakfast in the morning, she was sure that's what the professor would have wanted.

A thought suddenly struck Laura. "Juno."

"Y-es Laura."

"How did you know where to find us? How did you know we were in that cave?"

"It was the professor. Your granddad told him that you'd gone to discover something exciting. The professor guessed and told me where to look."

"Thank goodness for that. But I didn't know that he was coming to see me," said Laura. "He didn't write and tell me."

"It w-as urgent g-overnment business. I th-ink he has to go b-ack tonight."

Laura was disappointed to learn that the professor's visit would be so short.

They all arrived at Ginger's house first. He flew up the garden path leading to the front door and he started to tell his mum what had happened before she had time to close it behind him.

Just before they turned into Leanne and Lindsey's road, Laura asked if they would report Mr and Mrs Crookes to the police.

"'Course we will," Leanne said. "We'll tell Dad and he'll report it to Constable Pearson and tell him all about it. Constable Pearson will know what to do next."

"Thanks," replied Laura. "I just feel exhausted now," and she walked the rest of the way home hanging on to the arm of her invisible escort. When people heard her chattering away to no one, they looked at her askance and shook their heads. "Poor girl," they muttered. "Poor girl, how terribly, terribly sad."

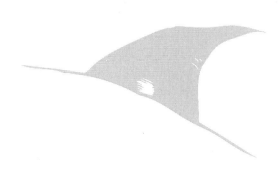

# CHAPTER SEVEN

## JUNO MAKES AN EVENING CALL
## – AND THE PROFESSOR MAKES A PROMISE

Mr and Mrs Crooks were staring at the stolen treasure that was lying on their dining room table. All that treasure, all that wealth. Did it make them feel any happier with one another, happier than they had been before? On the contrary, it seemed to have made things worse, they were almost coming to blows over how their ill-gotten gains should be shared.

"I want all the bracelets and the necklaces. In fact I want all of the jewellery," screamed Mrs Crookes. "I do, I want the lot."

She had been screaming at her husband like this for the best part of an hour.

Mr Crookes couldn't take any more. He'd had enough. He felt tired and defeated. He sighed; it was time to give in. "Alright, take everything that you want, woman, then please, will you leave me in peace?"

Recognising her victory, Mrs Crookes bared her teeth in a triumphant smile. She swept up all the jewellery, took it into her room and arranged it on the dressing table where she fondled it and drooled over it. Not knowing the difference between happiness and sheer avarice, Mrs Crookes thought this was the happiest day of her life.

Sadly for Mrs Crookes, this lovely feeling that had welled up inside her did not stay with her for long. She felt something cold tightening around her throat and it was almost choking her. Then came a voice, speaking to her from out of nowhere, a strange, metallic broken-up sort of a voice. "Child murd-erer. G-reedy, heartless woman, I am the ghost th-at will haunt you un-til the d-ay that you die – unless you con-fess."

The voice she heard was unlike any other voice she had ever heard before, it really sounded ghostly. Mrs Crookes almost collapsed with fear and then ran screaming to tell her husband about the ghost that was threatening to haunt her.

She entered the dining room expecting to see Mr Crookes trying to work out the value of the gold and silver that she had left for him on the table. But he wasn't where she expected and she shrieked again when she saw what had happened to him. Her husband was pinned by some invisible force to the dining room wall, his feet weren't touching the ground and his legs hung limp, flaccid and useless. Crookes was terrified and so was she.

Then came that awful voice again, speaking from out of nowhere, repeating the warning that it had given to her. Then suddenly, her husband was released and he fell to the floor. He lay there on his back, body twitching, helpless and whimpering.

Then, to their extreme horror, the couple saw that all the lovely treasure lying on the table was being spirited away and deposited back into the black plastic sack.

106

Mrs Crookes moaned, "It's the ghost, it's the ghost, it won't go away, it won't leave us alone – not ever!"

The ghostly nightmare, if that's what it was, hadn't quite finished. A few seconds elapsed and then items of jewellery from Mrs Crookes' bedroom came floating through the air into the dining room. Broaches, bracelets, necklaces and rings circled round the table, found the black plastic sack and disappeared inside it. Mrs Crookes fell to the floor beside her husband and began once again to scream with terror.

A dazed Mr Crookes felt the plastic sack being pressed into his hands. Then the ghostly voice commanded, "G-et to your f-eet. Take this to C-onstable Pearson in Tinsall village and c-onfess to your b-lack deeds. Go now! And if you f-ail to do so, I wi-ll haunt you f-or ever." The voice trailed away leaving a ghostly silence.

Mr and Mrs Crookes got to their feet, and for the first time in many, many years they held hands and together they stumbled out into the night to find Constable Pearson so they could confess their crimes to him.

The next day the professor visited Laura at her grandparents' cottage. "Gee, great to see you, Laura, and looking so well, too," he greeted her. And because it had been such a while since they had seen one another they spent quite a long time talking about old friends in San Francisco.

When they had finished reminiscing, the professor told Laura that Juno had informed him about the murderous couple who had locked them in the cave and left them to die.

"Pity they closed Alcatraz," he said. "It would have made an ideal home for them!"

"About the Roman treasure, Professor," said Laura, who didn't want to talk about those horrible Crookes people any more. But the professor interrupted her. "No, don't tell me. Let me guess. I know, you've decided to give it to Chester museum."

"How did you know?" said Laura.

"Because it's the right thing to do. And I know you will always do the right thing, Laura."

Laura blushed. "Thanks for trusting me, Professor."

Laura then went on to tell him about her new friends and how she had become the fourth Ponyteer and the vow they had taken to help people who needed help. The professor was most impressed. But he noticed that Laura began to look worried. He guessed at the source of her worry and he was right when he said, "It's about those stolen ponies, isn't it, that's what's making you unhappy?"

"Partly true," said Laura, and then the flood gates opened and she unburdened herself about Mrs Eastly and Alison's dream.

"That dream was dead spooky," she said, and she told him all about the little woman with the piercing eyes and how she had led Alison into the dark side of the hill.

When Laura had finished telling him about Alison's dream, the professor reminded Laura of the promise she had made to him in San Francisco, and Laura repeated her promise that she wouldn't go near to the place unless accompanied by him.

"What about Lindsey?" he asked.

"Oh, she won't go near the place, she's just as scared as Alison."

"And Leanne?" said the professor. "She strikes me as the sort of young woman who would be prepared to act independently."

"You're right about that, Professor. Leanne's very brave. She's the one who discovered who had stolen the ponies.

She's curious about what's going on under the hill, but she's given me her word that she won't go there without you."

"And will she keep her promise?"

"Oh, yes. Once Leanne has given her word, well – that's it."

The professor seemed satisfied with Laura's answers. He didn't ask any more questions and talked instead about some of the important things he had to do in America. Then he went on to tell her that he had leased a small workshop and flat just round the corner from the butcher's shop in Tinsall. He said, "With the help of Juno, I'm building a new and improved Jupiter – Juno will carry on with the work while I'm in the States."

"While you are in the States? But, but…you've only just arrived in England. Surely you're not leaving us already?"

"Tonight, my dear Laura, tonight. I have to. I've received some important information from friends in Britain. It's important for me to return to America without delay."

"Oh, I see," said Laura, sadly.

"Poor Juno, she'll be lonely when I'm away. Do you think that you and your fellow Ponyteers could visit her once in a while? She asked about you, especially, Laura."

"Of course I will. We'll all visit her," Laura promised. "We'll call often to keep her company."

"Good, then I give you my firm promise," said the professor. "On my next visit, and with the help of Juno and the son of Jupiter, and with you and the Ponyteers, we'll investigate the mystery of the dark side of the hill together."

He saw that Laura was misty-eyed. "What's this then, Laura, don't you believe me?"

"No, it's not that, Professor. It's just that we're all frightened. Dead scared of that Mrs Eastly. She's a witch,

Professor. When she gets out of prison she'll come and get us. Put a spell on us. Turn us into something horrid." Laura was on the verge of tears.

"Come, come, my dear Laura. Do you think I would leave you if I thought any harm would befall you? Never! I'm leaving Juno to protect you and your friends. Believe me, she's more than a match for Mrs Eastly. And Jupiter, soon the work on him will be complete. Between the two of them they will be stronger than a whole army of witches."

Laura felt ashamed and told the professor that she was sorry for doubting him.

He gave her a big reassuring hug and said, "Goodbye then, dear Laura, you'll be in safe hands."

The professor left the room and that was the last Laura saw of him until the next summer holidays.

# PART THREE

## THE DARK SIDE OF THE HILL

# CHAPTER ONE

## A LETTER FROM THE PROFESSOR

"Leanne! Lindsey!" – Laura's face was flushed with excitement as she burst in on the Farroll sisters, who were just finishing breakfast. She was holding a letter in her right hand and waving it above her head.

"What's up, Laura, practising semaphore?" Lindsey smiled before she popped a last piece of toast into her mouth.

Laura didn't reply; she was too excited to speak. She just stood there with the letter still held in her hand. Then she sat down between the two sisters, took a deep breath and said, "It's the best news – ever! Guess what? No, read it for yourselves, it's from the professor." She smoothed out the letter on the table and pointed a finger at the foot of the page; the professor's signature was there for all to see – Jules Klopstock – and it was underlined with a grand flourish from his pen.

"Wow!" exclaimed Leanne when she read the letter, "So he's keeping his promise then, the one he made to you last summer?"

"Sure is," replied Laura.

113

Leanne noticed that Laura's American accent hadn't altered one little bit even though she had lived in England for over a year. "I can't wait for him to come, Laura, I've been dying to find out what's going on up there." She pointed in the direction of Tinsall Hill. "Just think, Laura, after all these years, with the professor's help, we can now try to find out what's going on under the dark side of the hill."

"Not *try* to find out, Leanne. We *will* find out. That's what he's coming for. When the professor sets his mind to do something, he does it. He's that sort of guy."

Leanne was impressed; Laura had said exactly what she wanted to hear. "What do you think, Lindsey? If there are people living under the hill, we might be able to talk to them; maybe they are not as fierce as we imagine? For all we know, they could be quite nice."

Lindsey mockingly repeated what her sister had said, "For all we know, they could be quite nice." Then, speaking in her natural voice, she said, "Trust you to talk about them like that, Leanne. Always making excuses for people, that's you. You know very well that they're not like us, they're little monsters, that's what they are. And know something, Leanne, for all I care, they can stay under the hill and fight one another forever."

"But aren't you the slightest bit curious?" said Laura. "Surely there's something...?"

"No to both questions, Laura. That place is too scary. You won't catch me going anywhere near it and Alison won't go there, either. Besides, don't you think we've enough on our plate with old witch-face Eastly to worry about, without looking for any more trouble?" Lindsey's expression was serious. "I mean every single word, and I don't want to talk about..."

"Hey, hang on, Lindsey," said Laura, interrupting. "Look, Lindsey, we're all scared if it comes to that, but you'll have to talk about it sooner or later. Aw, c'mon, you'll have to, whether you like it or not."

"Oh, have to, will I?" said Lindsey, speaking in a sullen voice, "You going to tell me why?"

"Sure I will, if you promise to listen, okay?"

"Go on then."

"Well, we all know perfectly well that we've got a bunch of little monsters trying to kill one another right under our village hill and a wicked old witch who's just waiting her chance to get even – and you say you don't want to talk about it? For goodness sake, Lindsey, get real!"

Laura sounded quite angry and, because it was so unusual for Laura to show anger, Lindsey regretted having upset her.

"I'm sorry, Laura, about what I said just now. I didn't want to hurt you or Leanne, but I'm frightened, that's why I don't want to talk about it. And it's not fair, is it? Why did that horrible witch, Eastly, blame us when she was sent to prison? Wasn't our fault. And now she says she'll turn us into something nasty when she gets out. She'll try, you know, I know she will. And as for those little monsters that are fighting under the hill, well..." Lindsey's voice trailed off, she seemed to be on the verge of tears.

Leanne put a comforting arm round her younger sister. "Don't worry, Lindsey. Mrs Eastly can't get us. She can't hurt you. She's in prison, have you forgotten?"

"Of course I haven't forgotten, but, but..." Lindsey's voice faltered.

"I know how you're feeling, Lindsey," said Laura, sympathetically. "Perhaps Leanne has forgotten that witches have special powers and even if she's in prison she could still try to do us some harm."

115

"How can you say that, Laura? I haven't forgotten what witches can do. But you and Lindsey seem to have forgotten the most important thing of all."

"Oh, and what's that?"

"Juno," said Leanne. "You've forgotten Juno. I don't know why you're frightened, Juno's more than a match for a whole coven of witches. The professor told us that and I, for one, believe him."

Lindsey switched her gaze towards Laura when the professor's name was mentioned. "Leanne's right, Laura, isn't she?"

"Of course you are right. I don't know why I doubted. Juno will keep us safe, I know very well that she will."

"Does she know the professor's coming?" Leanne asked.

"Not yet. I wanted to tell you first."

Lindsey said, "Then don't you think that we should tell her, Laura, and while we're about it, tell her how scared we are of Witch Eastly? Well, that's what I'd like to do."

"I agree with Lindsey," said Leanne. "I reckon we should all go now and tell Juno. On the way, we could pick up Alison at the riding school."

"Suits me. Okay, c'mon then, you guys, let's go." Laura got to her feet. "The sooner we tell Juno what's happening the safer I'll feel."

"And me too!" Lindsey said, emphatically.

Laura gave Alison the professor's letter to read as they walked along to Juno's workshop.

"Who's this Mr Eliot Klopstock the professor mentions?" Alison asked, pointing to his name. They stopped to take a look.

Laura explained, "It's the professor's nephew. I first met

him in the States, ooh, must be about two years ago, now. He's very good looking."

"You're blushing, Laura," said Alison, teasing.

"Oh, he's too old," said Laura, sighing.

"How old?" asked Alison.

"Twenty-seven in January, I think."

"Old? He's positively ancient," said Leanne, adding, "Mind you, I thought the Eastly twins were good looking. Remember, Alison, we saw them on the day we went to Red House Farm and rescued the ponies? And much younger too, must be at least ten years younger than the professor's nephew." Then she laughed, "Pity, their stepmother's a witch." The colour on Lindsey and Alison's cheeks mounted when Leanne mentioned the Eastly twins, but Laura and Leanne didn't seem to notice.

"Is Mr Eliot brainy, like the professor?" Lindsey asked, deftly changing the subject.

"Well, there's not much he doesn't know about spaceships, rockets, robots and computers, if that's what you mean by being brainy," said Laura. "But I like his children's stories the best."

"Go on. What sort of stories?" Alison asked.

"Spooky, scary stories, about witches, mostly."

"You're joking!"

"I'm not. Surely everybody's read his latest story – *One Witch Too Many?*

There were blank faces all around except for Leanne's, and she said, "Is that the one where three witches are flying over the sea when a terrific storm blows up and makes them crash onto an island inhabited by monsters?"

"Yes," Laura nodded, and continued, "They're not injured in the crash but when they examine their broomsticks they find that two of them have been so badly damaged in the

117

crash, they are a complete write-off. The third one's okay, but it can take the weight of two people only. The three witches have to decide which one of them has to be left behind to face the monsters..."

"I get it, I get it – *One Witch Too Many* – great title," exclaimed Lindsey. "Pity the witch that they left behind wasn't our Mrs Eastly!"

Lindsey's remark made them laugh and for a while they forgot about the local monsters that were living under Tinsall hill.

When they reached the workshop, they found the door was unlocked. Juno had no use for locks, bolts and chains as a means of keeping her safe, she didn't need them. Juno had skills and powers that would out-match any kind of foe, and woe betide any one of them who had the nerve to try and put that to the test.

They entered the workshop to see the tiny light in the centre of Juno's forehead twinkle with delight as she recognised her visitors. After they had exchanged greetings, Juno said, "Come and s-ee where I'm up to with Jupi-ter, or should I s-ay son of Jup-iter?" She spoke to them in her metallic staccato voice and pointed to a motionless robot lying on the workshop table. A faint red light pulsed slowly in the centre of Jupiter's forehead.

"Is he...is he...?" Leanne did not quite know how to finish the question. She avoided using the word "alive". Somehow, when talking about a robot, it didn't seem to be the right word to use.

"Function-ing. Is that the word you are looking for, Leanne?"

"Yes, that's right, Juno – functioning," said Leanne. She thought the word functioning was very appropriate.

Juno said, "Yes, Jupiter is f-unctioning, but only to a degree. There's a b-it of work on him l-eft for me to do, the r-est is outside my c-apabilities, the p-rofessor will have to deal w-ith that."

"Ooh! That reminds me," said Laura, and she produced the letter from the professor and handed it to Juno.

After scanning the letter the robot handed it back to Laura. "I see that Mr El-iot w-ill be w-ith us to-morrow and the professor will arrive the day a-fter. That leaves me with j-ust enough t-ime to complete my work on J-upiter before they arrive – if I start to w-ork right now." There was something about Juno's voice that said "It's been nice seeing you and talking to you again, girls, but..!" The girls took the hint, said a quick goodbye and turned to take their leave. They had almost reached the door when Lindsey spun round and blurted out how much they feared Mrs Eastly.

Juno invited them to sit down again and then spoke to them slowly and calmly promising them that she would never let anything or anyone hurt them. They believed her. And when they left the workshop the Ponyteers felt confident and ready to face up to Mrs Eastly and whoever and whatever it was that lived under the dark side of the hill.

When they parted to go home, Laura promised she would phone the others to let them know when both Eliot and the professor arrived so they could all arrange to meet and discuss their plans.

Arriving home, Leanne would like to have shared with Lindsey some of the ideas that were buzzing around in her head about the creatures living under the hill. But she changed her mind, she could tell by the expression on her sister's face that she had heard quite enough for one day about witches and monsters, so she talked about Jupiter and Juno instead.

Lindsey was interested as soon as her sister brought up the subject. "The first Jupiter, the one in San Francisco, he wouldn't fly a rocket into outer space, would he?"

"No," said Leanne, "he wouldn't, he thought that it was a waste of money to fly what he called 'a giant fire-cracker' into outer space. That's how the trouble started. And it all ended up with poor Laura's mum and dad being killed in that terrible explosion."

"Poor, poor Laura, it must have been really awful for her," said Lindsey, sadly, and for a moment Leanne thought she would cry. Then, just as suddenly, Lindsey brightened up and said, "Well, I hope the son of Jupiter flies into outer space, I'd go with him like a shot, wouldn't you?"

"No, not on your life I wouldn't." Leanne's reply couldn't have been more emphatic.

That night, Laura lay in bed thinking about San Francisco and the friends she had left behind. And when she did fall asleep she dreamt about everything that had happened on the day her parents had been killed. In her dream she could see herself standing on the deck of the professor's house with Juno beside her. They were admiring the Golden Gate Bridge towering majestically above the water. Then the scene changed, and now she was sitting with Juno in the garden and shivering as the mist rolled in and made everything cold. She heard the loud explosion that killed her mother and father and injured the professor and the shock woke her up. When she eventually fell asleep again, her pillow was damp with tears.

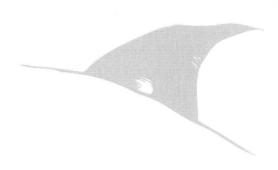

# CHAPTER TWO

## VISITORS FROM AMERICA

When Laura awoke next morning, the sun was shining in a clear blue sky and birds were singing. Bad dreams and anxious feelings were soon forgotten as she breathed the fresh warm air coming in from the Irish Sea and the west.

At the Farrolls', after breakfast, Lindsey said, "Come on, Leanne, let's sneak up on the tree platform to see what's happening at Laura's."

"You know what Dad said. He said it's too dangerous for all of us to go up there. We're too heavy."

"I'll go on my own then, I'm not too heavy. Don't tell Dad though." Without waiting for an answer Lindsey was up the ladder and standing on the platform. She got there just in time to see a car pulling up at Laura's cottage and in a dramatic voice, she announced, "This is Lindsey Farroll, reporting from Radio Tree House in Tinsall. The man from America that we've been waiting so patiently to see has just arrived in his car, folks. From where I'm standing, I have a perfect view of the scene. Yes! Yes! That's him, Mr Eliot Klopstock, nephew of the famous Professor Klopstock of San Francisco. The car door's opening. He is getting out of his car. Standing upright now, quite tall, six foot at a guess. There he goes. I can see him clearly from here, a handsome man with a black beard walking smartly up the path to Laura's cottage. He's at the door of the cottage. He's ringing the bell – the door's opening – he's going in – the door's closing behind him – it's closed! Well, listeners, you'll be pleased to learn that our long-awaited visitor from the United States has arrived safely in Great Britain and is now with his dear friend, Laura. And the residents of the village of Tinsall can at last breathe a sigh of relief, because when the professor arrives tomorrow he will be joining forces with his nephew and the intrepid Ponyteers to solve the mystery of the dark side of the hill. Stay tuned in and your favourite reporter, Lindsey Farroll, will keep you informed about the mission – from its beginning to its middle and to its final conclusion. So, it's goodbye from me, just now folks, and do have a good day!"

There was a smile on Leanne's face when Lindsey came down the ladder. "You know that you're completely bonkers, Lindsey, don't you?"

"I know," said Lindsey, with a false look of sadness on her face. "I must be a terrible problem for the family."

"Only joking," said Leanne. "You're the best sister in the world. Wouldn't swap you for anything." She put an arm round Lindsey and said they had better go into the house in case Laura phoned.

"How long do you think it will be before she rings?" asked Lindsey, her voice was serious now.

"Dunno, ten minutes, perhaps 20," said Leanne, "The professor's nephew has got to have time to say hello to Laura's granddad and gran first, before he even thinks of seeing us."

Almost exactly 20 minutes later, the telephone in the house rang. Lindsey took the phone off the hook before Leanne had time to get out of her chair.

"It's Laura," she whispered, with her hand held across the mouthpiece. "She wants to know if we can go down to the cottage, straight away?"

"Say we're on our way," said Leanne, "And I'll tell Mum so that she knows where we are."

Lindsey nodded. "Okay, Laura, we're on our way. Be with you in five minutes."

She put the telephone receiver back in its cradle and was half way to Laura's cottage before her sister overtook her.

Mr Eliot Klopstock was tall and slim with brown eyes. His black hair and beard were already flecked with grey. Laura did the introductions.

"Hi, you guys, pleased to meet you," he said, in a warm friendly voice.

"Hi, Eliot," they chorused. They liked him straight away.

After they had talked for a while, their visitor from the States said, "I've got some work to do with Juno tomorrow, it'll take 'til about ten in the morning, then how about this for an idea? Maybe I could hire a horse from the riding school and you could show me around the place? Get to know one another, okay? Buy you coffee and cake at the café on the hill later. We got a deal?"

The deal Eliot had proposed was accepted with great enthusiasm and after he had shaken each one of them by the hand Leanne said that she hoped his stay in England would be a very happy one. And to show that they liked him, they gave him four rousing cheers – "Because we're the four Ponyteers," they said.

123

He seemed to be very touched by this and said, "Thank you, guys, I appreciate that. Look forward to seeing you tomorrow then."

They set off just after ten o'clock the next day and it was clear from the way Eliot leapt into the saddle that he was a confident horse rider.

"Rides like a cowboy," said Lindsey, nudging Laura, "Only needs a couple of six shooters, slung low on the hip – and he'd be perfect."

They arrived at the Tea Pot Café just after eleven and tethered their horses under the large shady oak tree. The horses drinking trough was full to the brim.

It was already getting busy at the café and groups of hikers from the Sandstone Trail were arriving for an early lunch. The Ponyteers were scanning the garden for an empty table when Mrs Potts came to their rescue. She had one of her helpers bring out an extra table, some chairs and a large striped umbrella. Within minutes they were sitting comfortably round the table in a sheltered spot where they could keep an eye on their ponies.

"Perfect," said Eliot. "Just perfect." He smiled and waved his thanks to Mrs Potts. When she came back to take their order, they were talking about Professor Klopstock and as she was writing down the order, she hesitated and said, "I couldn't help overhearing the name Professor Klopstock. I don't wish to appear rude, sir, but could that be Professor Jules Klopstock you were talking about?"

"Sure," said Eliot. "Professor Jules Klopstock's my uncle, did you know him?"

"Yes, I know him. When I was a little girl he used to come and visit us at the café. He spent a lot of time digging on Tinsall Hill, near the Sandstone Trail. I remember him saying to me, "Rosie, one day I'll make the City of Chester even more famous than it already is. And he did. You should see all that treasure that's lying in the museum. And these young ladies," she beamed at the Ponyteers, "they helped him, they used his map and found it. Their photos were in all the papers, you know. But sorry, I'm talking too much, I'll get your order straight away, you must all be hungry." She hurried away, manoeuvring her ample figure skilfully between the tables.

"She'd be very good in the slalom," said Lindsey, who was watching her progress with interest.

Eliot laughed; he liked Lindsey's sense of humour.

"Mrs Potts. What a pleasant woman she is. Fancy remembering my uncle from all those years ago."

"Well, it's not all that surprising," said Alison. "Your uncle lived in Chester for five years after the war, apparently everybody knew him and liked him. And designing all those spaceships and robots and rockets has made him quite famous. D'you know the newspapers in England report everything that he says and does."

"Well then, we'll have to bring him to the Tea Pot Café at the earliest opportunity, won't we?" said the professor's nephew. He thought for a few seconds and added, "Gee, what a happy occasion that will be for him – and for Rosie too, I guess."

They didn't have long to wait before Mrs Potts returned with their order: a large tray laden with coffee, home made scones and cakes and dishes of fresh cream. She laid it on the table. "If you need anything else, just raise your hand and I'll be right over." They thanked her and off she went to attend to other customers.

The Ponyteers and Eliot were quiet after she left them; they were too busy munching away at the jam and cream-laden scones to talk. Very few words were said, until everything edible on the table had gone!

It was then that Leanne noticed Alison's normally pink cheeks were very pale. She was glancing anxiously in the direction of the door to the café.

"Goodness, Alison, what on earth's wrong?"

"It's her. It's her. I'm sure it's her," Alison whispered, nervously.

"Who, Alison, who is she?"

"That little woman working for Mrs Potts. See, she's standing by the door of the café, the woman with the pale wrinkled face? She was the one in my dreams, the one who helped me. I told you before about it, remember? I dreamt about her again, last night." Alison looked paler than ever.

"Try and forget about it, Alison, if it was only a dream." Lindsey didn't sound very sympathetic.

"But her eyes, Lindsey, they're so bright and strange..." Alison stopped talking. The little woman came over to their table, stacked the empty cups and dishes on a tray, put the bill on the table and left without saying a word.

"Did you see them? Did you see her eyes?" Alison whispered when she had gone.

Eliot said he couldn't remember ever seeing such bright piercing eyes before – not ever! And neither had any of the others. But the woman had a very kind face; they all agreed on that.

It was time to go and Eliot waved his hand to attract Mrs Potts' attention. She came straight over. After complimenting her on her home cooking and paying the bill, he mentioned how quiet but pleasant the little lady was who had cleared their table.

"She's foreign," Mrs Potts said. "I feel sorry for her, I think she's a refugee from somewhere in Europe. Works for me part-time; collects dishes, washes up, that sort of thing and as you say, very quiet but pleasant."

"Lives in Tinsall, does she?" asked Eliot, nonchalantly.

"I don't know for certain where she lives. I didn't ask, 'cos she can't speak much English. But I believe she lives in one of those old cottages near Red House Farm."

Eliot thanked her and said that he hoped to bring Professor Klopstock to see her one day in the not too distant future. Mrs Potts glowed with pleasure and told him how much she would look forward to that.

"What did you think of that?" asked Alison, when Mrs Potts had gone. "She said that little woman was foreign and couldn't speak much English. Funny, she spoke lots to me."

"Yes, Alison, but that was only in a dream, remember?" Lindsey repeated firmly.

"Lets leave it for now," said Eliot. "We can talk about it later. I promised to have the horse back at the stables by one o'clock." He looked at his watch. "Should be making a move I think."

Mrs Potts waved goodbye when they mounted their ponies. And as they rode away from the Tea Pot Café, the small woman with the strange piercing eyes moved out from the shadow of the door and watched them until they disappeared from view.

On their way home Alison said that she had promised her mum and dad that she would help to do some mucking out at the stables, so they should count her out of any plans for the rest of the day. Laura promised to phone her and Leanne and Lindsey as soon as the professor arrived.

Lindsey and Leanne were on a last warning from their mum to tidy up their rooms and it was best if they got it done before the professor arrived. That really worked out well for Laura and the professor's nephew as it gave them the rest of the day by themselves to catch up on news and chat about old times in San Francisco.

Before they all parted company, Leanne thanked Eliot for treating them to a very pleasant morning out and in return he was equally gracious and thanked them for having shown him around. He added that he hoped they would join him and the professor in a return visit to the Tea Pot Café in the not too distant future.

Everyone thought that was a great idea.

Lunch was not quite ready when Leanne and Lindsey arrived home, so they watched their young brother, Alex, and his friend, Ginger Tomkins, playing marbles on the patio. The two boys were so engrossed in their game they were totally unaware of the girls' presence. Lindsey wasn't the least bit interested in the strategy or the tactics of their game, but her attention was drawn to the marbles. The sun was shining on them, making them sparkle like precious stones.

"Funny looking marbles, those. What do you think, Leanne?"

Leanne watched the boys playing with the marbles for a moment, then she realized what they actually were. "They're not marbles at all, Lindsey, they're..."

"Part of the Roman treasure that we found in the cave," interrupted Lindsey.

"Alex!" she yelled and the air vibrated. Alex cocked his head in her direction, "What do you want, Lindsey?"

"May I see some of your lovely marbles, Alex," she coaxed sweetly.

"Sure," he said, handing her some to look at. "Cool, eh?" he said, proudly, as Lindsey examined the marbles.

"Where did you get these?" she asked in the most casual voice she could manage.

But Alex wasn't fooled; he saw a light in her eyes that told him the tone of her voice wasn't sincere. In a flash he grabbed the marbles from his sister's hand and buried them deep in his pocket. "We got them from the cave, and they're ours, where do you think we got them from?"

"Well, they're not marbles. They should be in the museum with the rest of the treasure," said Lindsey, sharply, adding, "I'm going to tell Dad."

Alex stuck out his tongue at Lindsey and made for the garden gate with Ginger. "Where do you think you two are going?" his sister demanded.

"Ginger's, to get something to eat. And where there aren't any girls there to boss you about, so that's where we're going." And having said that, Alex and Ginger darted through the garden gate and out of sight.

Leanne smiled. Lindsey groaned. "Boys," Lindsey said. "Boys are simply terrible. And that one, our Alex, he's the worst one of the lot."

The next day Laura phoned as promised. She told them that the professor had arrived, but it would take him about two days to do some important work on Jupiter. In the meantime, she and her grandparents were showing Eliot around Chester and the old church in Bunbury. She apologised and said that she would get back to them soon.

Laura was as good as her word. Two days later, just after breakfast, she was on the phone again. She sounded very excited. "The professor's finished his work on Jupiter, and he wants to see you at the workshop. Eliot's here as well. I've already phoned Alison."

Leanne and Lindsey arrived at the workshop within minutes of Laura putting the phone down.

Eliot was sitting in a corner between Juno and the new

robot – Jupiter. He gave the girls a friendly wave as they came in. "Hi girls, glad to see you again," he called.

Alison had arrived before them. She stopped chatting to Laura and came across to say hello. There weren't enough chairs to go around so they perched up on the workshop table beside Laura.

Professor Klopstock was pacing up and down the room, looking very thoughtful. Every time he moved to turn around, his artificial leg squeaked. And every time this happened, Juno put a hand over her mouth and gave a little metallic giggle. The professor pretended to be angry. "Just listen, everyone, do you hear Little Miss Squeaky Legs, she's laughing at me, y' know. I don't know why she's laughing 'cos her legs squeak a darn sight more than mine." Everybody laughed, happy because the professor and Juno were allowing them to share in what was their little private joke.

The professor stopped his pacing up and down and began to address them. "First of all, I want to introduce you all to the son of Jupiter." He waved an arm in the direction of a robot sitting in the corner of the workshop, between Eliot and Juno. Jupiter Junior stood up, gave a little bow, raised an arm to acknowledge what the professor had said and then sat down again.

Laura asked, "Please can we see if Jupiter can become invisible, just like Juno?"

"Of course you can, my dear," said the professor and smiled. "That is, if Jupiter cares to oblige."

Jupiter stood up. "Hey, that invis-ible stuff, now th-at's real coo-l, Pro-fessor. I like doing that 'here he is and n-ow he's gone' trick!" He slid back a little panel on his arm and pressed a button. Without any shimmering or shaking, in an instant, Jupiter had gone – vanished completely!

Everyone clapped wildly, none more wildly than Juno, who clanked her metal hands together noisily. Then there was silence and the professor pretended to look anxious. He ran nervous fingers through his thick white beard. "Where is he? I hope he hasn't gone forever, I hope he'll come back," he said. Pivoting round on his squeaky leg he called, "Jupiter, where are you? Where are you, Jupiter?"

"R-ight, r-ight here, Professor. Cool man, eh?" Jupiter had appeared as quickly as he had disappeared and he was standing behind the professor. Again they all applauded.

Lindsey whispered to Alison, "Jupiter's talking like Juno – but sounds even more American. If Alex hears him he'll start talking like him. I can just hear him now, 'Real cool, man!' "

Jupiter returned to his seat between Eliot and Juno. He was pleased that his vanishing performance had functioned so well.

"He's the son of Jupiter, all right," said the professor, still smiling. "But I think we'd better call him Jupiter from now on, it's much easier on the tongue. Jupiter's part of the team, a very important member, and we welcome him most warmly."

Professor Klopstock continued with the news they were all waiting to hear. "Last year I made a promise to the Ponyteers and this year I intend to keep it. I said then that I would return to Tinsall and with their help would investigate and solve the mystery of the dark side of the hill. Well…" he paused dramatically, "that time has come – we start our investigation today! This afternoon we will set up our headquarters at Red House Farm!"

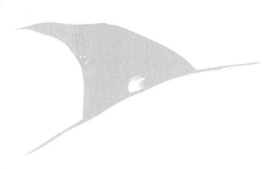

# CHAPTER THREE

## REDHOUSE FARM REVISITED

In the afternoon the girls ran up the stairs at Red House Farm to take a look out of Mrs Eastly's bedroom window. The dark side of the hill seemed very near and more decayed than ever. There was something about that part of the hill that scared Alison, but today it seemed more menacing than ever, and although it was a very warm day her skin began to feel cold. She raised her eyes to scan the Sandstone Trail higher up the hill. There, she could see groups of hikers walking along the sandy path and through the open window she could hear them singing and laughing. The sound raised Alison's spirits again and helped her relax a little, even though she was standing in Witch Eastly's bedroom!

Leanne drew Alison's attention to Eliot and the two robots working on the hill. Jupiter and Juno were driving thin metal spikes into the ground and Eliot was attaching something to them.

"I wonder what they are doing?"

Before anyone could answer, they heard the professor's leg squeak. No one had seen him enter the room. "They're installing special microphones, Leanne. And when that's

132

done we'll be able to monitor and record every sound that's made on the hill."

"Under, as well as on top of the hill, Professor?" Alison asked him.

"Sure, well, that's what my nephew tells me and he's an expert in matters such as this, so I believe him, okay?" The professor stopped talking and rubbed his eyes. The scar under his left eye, the one injured in the San Francisco explosion, was inflamed and sore looking.

Still rubbing his eye, he walked over to a large wooden chest, which was standing close to the window. He lifted the lid, and found that it was empty. "Good, good," he said. "Now come along with me, girls, you can give me a hand, okay?" And he led them downstairs and into the kitchen where boxes of equipment were piled up on the table.

But before they started to unpack the contents of the boxes, Laura asked him a question about something they were all eager to know. "Why are we working from this place, Professor, I mean, Red House Farm, of all places? Why choose the house where Witch Eastly lived? A lot of bad, frightening things happened here."

"Sorry, sorry, Laura, my fault," the professor said, lifting his hands in apology. "I should have explained it to you more fully at the meeting. Red House Farm is the perfect forward observation post, perfect for what we have in mind. If you can think of anywhere with a better vantage point, tell me about it, and we'll see what we can do." No one replied, no one could think of a better place. Professor Klopstock continued with his explanation. "When I called on the estate agents they offered me this place to rent. So I took up their offer and rented it for a month. I guess Mrs Eastly needs the money to meet legal fees, apart from anything else. She seems set to be in prison and her stepsons in a remand centre for quite some time yet. But without being asked, the estate agents informed me that Mrs Eastly wouldn't sell the house; they said she was adamant about that. Don't know why. Well, that's about all, I guess. Any more questions?"

Nobody spoke. "Okay then," said the professor, "Let's get this stuff upstairs, there's a lot of work to be done."

It took them over an hour to get all the equipment safely upstairs and then under the professor's supervision, they assembled everything exactly the way he wanted it to be.

Then the professor pressed a switch on what looked like a television set, which he had placed on the large heavy chest near the window. Instantly the set purred into life.

Lindsey was curious, "What's that for?"

"Remember that piece of equipment we placed inside this chest, underneath this screen, Lindsey? Well, that piece of equipment is a computer. It's a very special computer. My nephew invented it. That computer and the screen work in unison."

"But how do they work together, what do you mean?" said Lindsey."

The professor looked out of the window to see that his nephew and the two robots were returning to the house. "They've just planted five microphones on the hill, Lindsey. Special microphones, highly sensitive, they can pick up sounds from deep down inside the hill as well as well as on the surface."

"Isn't that what you were telling us about, Professor?"

"That's right, Leanne, but there's more to it than that. To put it simply, speech sounds in any language can be interpreted by the computer and displayed on this screen, instantly translated into English – *English*, got that?"

"Wow" said Laura. "Does that mean they'll be able to understand what we say to them?"

The professor looked doubtful. "No, we can't have two-way dialogue with this apparatus; we can monitor what they say, interpret it and put it on the screen, that's okay. But to carry out a one-to-one conversation, now that would be a more complex operation, which requires two of these." He held up a sort of helmet-shaped object, something that looked like a footballer's head protector. "They would have to wear one of these," he said.

"How would that work," puzzled Alison, who was finding it difficult to follow all this technical information.

"Thought transference," replied the professor, "And before you ask, let me tell you how that works, okay?"

He gave a little tug at his beard before he spoke and looked at Lindsey. "I think maybe a demonstration would be the best way to explain how thought transference works. D'you want to try it out, Lindsey, with your sister, Leanne?"

"I'd love to," said Leanne.

"Won't hurt, will it?" said Lindsey, who was a bit scared of the weird-looking helmet.

The professor smiled. "Hurt you? Not one little bit, Lindsey. Put them on, neither of you say a word and we'll just watch the screen to see what happens."

Leanne put on her headgear and Lindsey reluctantly followed suit. Everyone watched expectantly. Then the screen flashed up the text of what Lindsey was thinking. Laura and Alison and Leanne read Lindsey's thoughts about Alex and Ginger Tomkins and the precious jewels they had been using as marbles. "If you don't take them to the museum, Alex, then I'll report you to my dad."

Leanne watched intently as her own thought response was texted onto the screen. "Never mind the marbles, this equipment is amazing, just amazing!"

"Demonstration successful, I think," said the professor. "Thank you, Leanne and Lindsey, my nephew will be pleased."

"I am pleased," said Eliot, who had been standing unnoticed in the back of the room. "But there's just one more thing to add. The print-out on the screen has to be expressed simultaneously in both languages if the two people conversing speak different languages, otherwise it would be goodbye to a two-way conversation, wouldn't it?"

"And can it do all that? " said Laura, with awe in her voice."

"Of course," said Eliot, modestly. "That's the way it works. Quite simple, really."

When Leanne and Lindsey removed their headgear the professor laid a large new journal on Mrs Eastly's dressing table, which they were using as a makeshift desk. "This is the log book," he said. Then he explained how they should record in it to sign on and off duty when it came to their turn to do a watch. "Every incident should be timed, dated and logged fully in the book."

"What do you mean when it comes to our turn to do a watch?" asked Laura.

The professor explained that he wanted two girls to be on daytime watch between the hours of ten in the morning and one in the afternoon. The other two to be on duty between one o'clock and four in the afternoon. "In other words the day will be split into two watches, Laura."

Laura nodded her head to indicate that she understood.

Professor Klopstock reassured them that one of the robots would always be there on duty, day or night, and the girls could decide who it was they came on watch with and could change partners whenever they liked to suit their own activities.

Finally, he told them that he or Eliot would be popping in at frequent intervals to monitor the situation.

"What about me and Ginger?" exclaimed Alex. He and his friend had managed to sneak into the house unobserved and creep upstairs. "Why can't we go on watch?"

The professor pretended to take Alex's question very seriously and for a few seconds appeared to be deep in thought. Then he asked Alex solemnly, "Do you and Ginger think you would be capable of taking charge of the rations, Alex? Do you think you could handle such an important task?"

Alex shuffled his feet. He felt flattered by the suggestion of importance, but to tell the truth he really didn't have a clue what the professor had been talking about. He decided to ask a question of his own. "What do you mean, rations?"

The professor smiled. It was clear from his smile that he enjoyed Alex and Ginger's company. "Now, rations, Alex. It means that you have to look after the chocolate, tea and coffee and fruit drinks, make sure the supplies don't run out. Oh! And I almost forgot, you'll have to make sure you have a stock of your favourite drink. I forget the name, remind me, Alex?"

"Dynamite!" cried Alex and Ginger, together."

"Could you do that important job then?" asked the professor.

"Easy," said Alex.

"Yeah, dead easy," said Ginger.

"Good, then that's settled," said the professor. "All you need now is a float."

"Float!" Alex said, wondering what else the ration job entailed. "We don't have to catch fish, do we?"

The professor laughed. "Not that kind of a float Alex," He explained to Alex what a money float was. "I'll always make sure that your float will never fall below five pounds, that's the amount of money I'm going to put on the silver tray over there, okay? Oh, and just one more thing, I want you and Ginger to accompany your sister, whichever one it is, to Red House Farm, whenever they are on duty. In that way I know they will be in safe hands."

The thought that he and Ginger were being given responsibility for looking after the girls made them feel very grown up. Filled with enthusiasm they agreed to do everything the professor had asked.

Leanne thought that the professor had been very clever and understanding in the way that he had involved Alex and Ginger and Lindsey realised that the professor had made those arrangements for the boys to accompany the girls so that the girls could keep Alex and Ginger out of mischief. What a wise old professor he is, thought Lindsey.

The professor deposited five one-pound coins in the silver tray as a float and asked the girls to keep a written record of how much was spent and on what.

Alex took one of the pound coins from the tray to buy sweets and chocolate for the next day and Leanne dutifully entered this in the book. Then she and Laura signed "on duty" in the logbook.

All the others went home, except for Jupiter. He began patrolling the area between Red House Farm and the dark side of the hill, guarding the special microphones and making sure the girls were safe.

# CHAPTER FOUR

## MRS EASTLY HAS PRISON VISITORS

Mrs Eastly paced up and down in her prison cell. She couldn't settle. She was angry. She was in prison and it was all because of those Ponyteers – especially the one who had laughed at her when she crawled out of the muddy stream and called her a monster from the deep. "Monster of the deep," she muttered, "I'll give her monster of the deep. Just wait 'til I get out of here and then I'll show her. And that other one, that one from America as well, oh yes, I know all about you, young lady. Just you wait and you'll get it as well."

She was still muttering when "Lights Out" was called, and everything was plunged into darkness. Mrs Eastly wasn't sleepy, she was angry, so she lay down on her bed, plotting and planning her revenge. She looked at her wristwatch to check the time but it was too dark to see the dial. She heard a noise at the window, a tap- tapping sound. The witch got out of her bed to investigate. She peered out of the window and into the gloom and could hardly believe what she saw. Close to the window were two women's faces and, bobbing up and down as though in a boat, they were grinning at her through the glass. But they weren't in a boat, she realised, they were her sister witches and they were hovering outside the window, bobbing about astride their broomsticks!

"Hi, Sister Bertha," they called. She could hear them quite distinctly through the air vent in the window.

"Hi girls," she called back to them, "am I glad to see you."

The bobbing up and down continued. Mrs Eastly squinted through the glass. "We haven't met before, have we?"

"No, we haven't," they answered. "But you might have seen us perform, we're part of the aerobatics team. Sister Mabel is our commandant. We were on patrol in the area when we got a call from Control who instructed us to call on you to see how you were faring."

Bertha smiled, baring her yellow teeth, "Thanks, girls, thanks for coming. Tell everybody I'm fine."

"Okay, will do," said one of the witches. Bertha Eastly assumed she was the one in charge.

"But hey, Bertha," she said, "You must be pretty important for Control to ask us to make a special call to see you?"

"Well, it's good to know somebody's thinking about me," said Mrs Eastly, grimly. Then, in an afterthought, she asked, "You coming to see me again?"

"'Course, if you want us to. But where's your witches' mobile phone? On your WMP you can call us any time, day or night. Yeah, just give us a call on that, okay."

"It's still in the house at Red House Farm," replied Mrs Eastly, testily. "I left it behind by mistake."

"Oh dear," said the leader. "Does that mean that anyone wandering into the house could find it?"

" 'Course they couldn't. You take me for an idiot?" Mrs Eastly retorted, angrily. "It's in my secret den. Nobody will find it there."

"Good," said the leader. "Here, take mine for now and use it, okay? I can easily get a replacement." She slipped her WMP through the air vent to Mrs Eastly. "If you want to call me, just press this button and call Red Leader, okay?"

Mrs Eastly noted the button Red Leader had indicated and thanked her profusely.

"That's okay, think nothing of it," said Red Leader and she pointed to the witch who was bobbing up and down beside her, saying, "This is Red One, my deputy. There are five of us in the team, but I instructed the others to return to base; two's enough to just say hello. These days we have to think economy, don't we? After all, those broomstick-flying hours cost money. Expensive! Yes, sister Bertha, we've got to cut down on costs, okay?"

All this talk about economy and the way Red Leader spoke – okay this and okay that – put Mrs Eastly off her completely. But she wanted something from her, so she managed to hold her tongue. She asked Red Leader ingratiatingly, "I know you're frightfully busy and have such an important and demanding job, but I wonder, Red Leader, if you could possibly find time to do a little something for me?"

"Anything you want, Sister," Red Leader laughed, "As long as you don't want money, okay?"

Mrs Eastly almost groaned – another "okay"! She closed her eyes and winced. When she opened them again, she noticed that the sky had brightened considerably. Most of the cloud cover that had darkened the sky had disappeared and now the moon was shining through the gaps. It was light enough for her study her visitors more closely.

They weren't wearing black pointed hats – that was the first thing Mrs Eastly noticed. Instead, they were wearing heavy goggles and some kind of helmet, not unlike motorcyclists' gear. A lamp formed an integral part of the helmet – flush fitting – specially designed to reduce in-flight drag. A small metal arm curved down from a point near the right ear on the helmet to hold a tiny microphone close to the lips. Mrs Eastly was aghast. She pointed to the helmet and goggles and demanded to know why they were improperly dressed.

The two witches nearly fell off their broomsticks, laughing. "Where've you been these past few years, Grandma? If you'd been reading..."

They didn't get any further. Mrs Eastly exploded with anger, "Don't you dare Grandma me," she yelled. "And if you want to remain in the aerobatics team, then you better start showing me some respect. Sister Mabel, your commandant, is my cousin. So you see, I have friends in very high places, that's why you were sent here to see me."

Red Leader and Red One looked uneasily at one another. "Sorry, Sister Bertha, sorry. We meant no offence." Then they went on to say that the wearing of helmets was now compulsory – the order came out three years ago. "It's in all the Witches' Publication Amendments," they said.

Mrs Eastly had many faults and laziness was one of them. Her WPAs lay in bundles, unopened in her den. She had been too lazy to read any Publication Amendments for at least the past five years!

Her reaction was defensive. "I've been ill, you know. I haven't had the energy to read my Amendments for ages. And my stepsons, the twins, now they've been a real handful, you don't know what I've had to put up with." She lied to her visitors and told them that the twins had stolen some ponies and put the blame on her and that was how she had come to be locked up in prison.

Red Leader and Red One were very understanding when they heard Mrs Eastly's story and explained to her that the lamp on their helmets came in very useful for making bad weather landings and in making night searches after crash landings.

"Crash landings, do you get many of those?" Mrs Eastly asked nervously.

"Mostly in the aerobatics team," said Red Leader. "Expect that's what lead to the wearing of these silly helmets, okay."

Mrs Eastly's feelings towards Red Leader softened slightly when she described the helmets as silly. "And what's that funny thing that seems to be growing from your ear to your mouth looking like it wants to be eaten?"

"Microphone," replied Red Leader. "Just a press of a button, that's all it takes, and I can speak to any member of my team. Press another one and I'm speaking to Control. Another one and I'd be talking to you – simple, okay?"

Mrs Eastly realized how out of date she had allowed herself to become. She changed the subject. "My estate agent tells me that Red House Farm has been rented to a Professor Klopstock for a month. Don't know anything about him, except he's American..."

Red Leader filled in his details, "He's an archaeologist. He's got permission to do some digging up on Tinsall Hill. He's..."

Mrs Eastly interrupted, "Well, I'd like you to keep an eye on him for me, tell me what's going on." She looked Red Leader right in the eye and said, sarcastically, "*Okay?*"

The jibe was lost on Red Leader and she replied agreeably, "Okay, sister Bertha, we'll give you our first report tonight. Back before midnight, okay?"

"Okay," said Mrs Eastly, wearily.

Red Leader pressed a button and spoke into her microphone, "Red One from Red Leader, prepare for immediate take-off."

"Red Leader." was the curt acknowledgement.

"Go! Go! Go! Tallyho!" Red Leader called, and she blasted off into the night, hotly pursued by Red One.

Bertha Eastly gasped when she witnessed the speed of their departure. She staggered and fell onto her bed. And there she lay feeling utterly exhausted and some unwelcome thoughts came into her head, telling her that perhaps Bertha Eastly was getting rather old, and she questioned her own ability to continue performing effectively as a witch.

# CHAPTER FIVE

## RED HOUSE FARM
## UNDER AIR SURVEILLANCE

Leanne was tired when she came off watch and after her evening meal went to bed early. But she didn't sleep. She lay awake thinking about the thought transference equipment and how dangerous it would be if it fell into the wrong hands. No wonder the professor had made them promise not to breathe a word about it to anyone.

The moon came out from behind a bank of clouds and made her room as bright as day. She got out of bed and went into Lindsey's room. "You awake, Linz?" she whispered.

"Yeah," came the sleepy reply. "What do you want, Leanne?"

"Had a feeling something was happening up at Red House Farm. Can't get it out of my head. Mind if I look through your window, I can see it better from there."

"S'okay, Leanne," Lindsey yawned. "Think I'll take a look, too."

Lindsey got out of bed and joined her sister at the window.

"Wow! Did you see that, Lindsey?" Leanne was rubbing her eyes. "There were two of them, Linz, silhouetted against the moon – on their broomsticks. I've never seen anything fly as fast as that!"

Lindsey had seen them but she was too busy pinching herself to see if she was awake to give an immediate reply. Then she said, "Look! Look! Leanne, they're coming back, coming back the opposite way. Fly any lower and they'll crash into those trees."

It was a sight never to be forgotten and both Leanne and Lindsey were amazed, but they would have been amazed even more had they been able to hear the conversation that was taking place between the two witches on their broomsticks…

"Red Leader to Red One – how do you read, over?"

"Loud and clear, Red Leader."

"Red Leader to Red One, check altimeter. Going in for a low-level photographic run. Red House Farm three miles ahead. Followed by a reciprocal run, over."

"Red Leader from Red One, understood, over and out."

The witches adjusted their height and speed and switched on their photographic equipment. It was true, they were flying very low. When Red Leader said low-level run, she really meant it. They were almost scraping the treetops when they took their photographs.

"Nicely done, Red One," said Red Leader. "Evasive practise now, then we'll go home. You ready, Red One?"

"Red Leader from Red One, ready."

"Red Leader on course for base, corkscrew right, Go! Go!"

When the corkscrew exercise had been completed Red Leader congratulated Red One, "Oh, very well done, Red One. Perfect. Back to base now. Don't know about you, but I'm starving."

Leanne and Lindsey were spellbound. "I don't know what they were up to flying over Red House Farm," said Lindsey, "but you've got to hand it to them, they can really fly those broomsticks!"

After they had landed at headquarters, Red Leader borrowed Red One's WMP and phoned Sister Bertha in prison to tell her they would deliver their infra-red photos to her just as soon as they had them developed. Mrs Eastly was impressed.

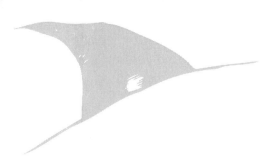

# CHAPTER SIX
## ALEX AND GINGER MAKE A DISCOVERY

The following afternoon, Leanne and Laura set off on foot to relieve Alison and Lindsey, who were on the morning watch. Accompanied by Alex and Ginger, they stopped at the corner shop and the boys went inside to replenish their rations with one of the pound coins taken from the float. They came out of the shop pleased with the sweets they had purchased and boasted they had three pence change.

"I'll put the change in the tray with the other money, when we get to Red House Farm," said Alex.

"And don't forget, Laura, it's got to be logged in the book," said Ginger, seriously.

Leanne and Laura complimented the boys, saying it was clear that the professor had made a sound choice when he gave them the responsibility for the rations.

Once the girls had relieved Alison and Lindsey and signed on watch, they looked out of the window to see if Jupiter was on patrol. He was, they could see him across the farmyard near the old shed.

"Y'know what, Laura, when Jupiter did that disappearing trick and then popped up unexpectedly behind the professor's back, I thought it was so funny."

"Well, he's different from the first Jupiter, I'll grant you that; seems to have a sense of humour," said Laura. "Did you notice, Leanne, the professor hasn't given this Jupiter a self-destruct button?"

Leanne realized they had strayed into a very sensitive area, so she dropped Jupiter as a subject for discussion. She said, "D'you think we should monitor the screen to see if anything's happening on the hill?"

Laura agreed, took a bite at a piece of chocolate and then took turns with Leanne to keep an eye on the screen. Nothing happened, the screen remained blank.

"Looks like we're in for a boring watch," said Leanne.

"In that case, Alex and Ginger might as well go home, there's nothing here for them to do. Do you want to go home, boys?" Laura asked.

"No, we'll play around here for a while and go home with you and Leanne when your shift's over," said Alex.

"Please yourselves," said Leanne. It was then that she noticed that her brother had a coil of rope in his hands. It looked very much like the clothesline she had used to help in the escape from Red House Farm. "Where did you get that?" she asked.

"Somebody had tied it to the kitchen door," he said. "Now why would somebody want to do a daft thing like that?"

Leanne replied, "I know who that daft person was, Alex. But it's a long story. Remind me to tell you about it one day."

"Okay, Leanne, you can tell me when we get home tonight." Alex seemed quite content to leave it at that.

"Aw, come on, Alex, don't let's hang about, it's dead boring here." Ginger was holding the door open. "You coming?"

Before Laura or Leanne could say anything the boys were through the bedroom door and had disappeared from sight.

Leanne shook her head. "Let's hope they manage to keep out of trouble." Then she added, "Now we're by ourselves we could try on those thought transference helmets without being disturbed. What do you think, Laura, shall we – see if they work?"

"Why not? Guess it gives us something to do."

The girls put on the headgear and plugged them into the computer. Immediately the screen displayed a printed message in English, which said, "I wonder why Laura didn't give me a piece of her chocolate?"

They exploded with laughter and took off their helmets. "It works! It really works, even if it does prove that I'm a greedy monster," Laura said.

They were still chuckling about that when Leanne said that perhaps they shouldn't play around with the helmets again in case it took their minds off what they were supposed to be doing. Laura agreed that it was important they didn't miss anything that was taking place on the hill.

Half an hour elapsed. Still nothing on the tube, it remained blank. Everything was quiet on the hill. Leanne and Laura resigned themselves to a long boring watch.

"Laura, if I tell you something, promise you won't laugh?"

"C'mon, you've got to tell me, Leanne. I promise not to laugh." Laura looked excited

Leanne began to tell Laura about the two witches she and Lindsey had seen the previous night when they were looking through the bedroom window. As the story unfolded Laura began to look more and more frightened. Finally, she said, in a trembling voice, "You don't think old witch face, Eastly, sent them to find us, do you?"

"No, I think it's just a coincidence, Laura. I think those witches were out on some sort of training flight and had nothing to do with Mrs Eastly at all."

"Think we should do something about it, Leanne?"

"Not much we can do really, keep our eyes skinned, tell Juno what's happened, and that's it."

"How long before Witch Eastly gets out of prison?" asked Laura.

"Don't know for sure. Not until this time next summer, at least that's what I've been told. But don't worry, no matter when she gets out, Juno will be there to protect us."

"All the same, I wish they'd keep her there forever, I'd feel a lot happier then," said Laura.

Meanwhile, Alex and Ginger were downstairs in the large entrance hall of the farm house. Alex was toying with one end of the rope; the rest was still coiled round his arm.

Ginger eyed the rope in Alex's hand and said, "What you going to do with that then, Alex?"

Alex was counting the number of coat pegs on either side of the hall when he heard Ginger ask the question and straight away an idea came into his head. "Tell you about the rope if you let me borrow your pocket-knife, Ginger. Mine's blunt. Laura blunted it when she tried to dig us out of the cave."

Ginger produced his pocket-knife and handed to Alex. "It's nice and sharp, be careful."

Alex cut the rope into several lengths and then handed the pocket-knife and a couple of rope lengths to Ginger.

151

"Now what?" said Ginger.

"Tie one end of your rope to one of the coat pegs on your side, Ginger, then tie the other end to one of the pegs on my side. Then when you've done that, do the same thing with the other piece. Okay?"

"Okay," said Ginger, and he set about completing his task.

Alex set to work too, and soon there were four pieces of rope stretching from one side of entrance hall to the other.

"Now what?"

"Now we can play Tarzan," said Alex. "Swing from one rope to the other. Don't fall off though, Ginger. That river underneath these ropes is full of crocodiles. Fall off and they'll tear you to pieces and chew you up for dinner."

"Bags me first then," called Ginger and before Alex could argue, his pal was half way across the dangerous river calling out, "Great Alex! Great! Come on, why don't you have a go?"

Twisting his body round for a repeat run and still swinging on the ropes like Tarzan, Ginger noticed that Alex was standing rooted to the spot, staring with eyes and mouth wide open. Ginger couldn't understand why Alex wasn't sharing the fun. "What's up, Alex, you look daft staring like that. Come on, come on, you'll like it. Come on, you have a go."

At last Alex managed to get his mouth working and pointing with a shaky hand, he said, in a voice that was barely above a whisper, "See the wall on the side, Ginger, see the wall."

Ginger looked at the wall to his left-hand side, released his grip on the rope he was holding and fell bottom down into the crocodile infested river.

"It's that coat peg that did it," said Alex, who had now

got over the shock. He pointed to the coat peg. "It moved when you swung on it and opened that secret panel."

Ginger took a nervous look at the gap in the wall. "What do you think we should…?"

"Go in and take a look," said Alex. "I think that what we've discovered is Witch Eastly's secret den."

"I'm not sure about that, Alex. Don't you think we should ask Leanne and Laura first?"

Alex moaned. "Aw, c'mon, Ginger. Leanne's the last one to ask. You know what she'd say, she'd say the room's private, or dangerous, or both! One way or another, she'd stop us from going in."

"Well, you go in first then, seeing as you're so keen."

"All right then, I will." And Alex stepped boldly into the den, saying, "Don't worry, Ginger, the witch can't hurt us, she's still in prison – remember?"

Ginger counted slowly to ten, and then, moving even more slowly, he followed Alex into the den.


Upstairs, Leanne and Laura were gradually getting more and more bored. It didn't improve matters either, when Laura's grandma called her on her mobile to tell her that the professor was going to take Alison and Lindsey for a walk to the café on top of the hill and then have afternoon tea with them. "Says it will test his tin leg," Laura's grandma laughed.

Now the girls felt jealous as well as bored.

Laura looked at her wristwatch. "Nearly three," she sighed.

"Hmm. They'll just be arriving at the Tea Pot Café now," said Leanne, trying her utmost to sound unconcerned.

Suddenly a burst of loud shouting came up from the bottom of the stairs.

"Help! Help! Leanne, Laura. Come as quick as you can, help, help..."

The voice trailed off as an ashen-faced Ginger Tomkins burst into the room. "Help! Help!" he repeated, whilst tugging at Leanne's arm.

"What on earth is it, Ginger? What's wrong?" Leanne put an arm round him to try and calm him down. Ginger shrugged her off. "No, no, Leanne, you've got to go downstairs and rescue Alex, he needs your help, now. Come on!"

"If this is one of your jokes, Ginger Tomkins...?"

"No, no, it's Alex, he's stuck to the ceiling in Witch Eastly's secret den."

"Oh, you young monkey!" said Leanne. "You and Alex must have made it up. Fancy expecting me to believe such a wild story as that."

Ginger was now almost beside himself with worry. He turned to Laura. "You believe me, Laura, don't you? Alex is pinned to the ceiling by a broomstick we found in Witch Eastly's den."

This time the girls believed him. "If you stay here and monitor the screen, Laura, I'll go to help my brother. Come on, Ginger, quick now, lead the way, don't worry, I'm coming, I'm coming."

Ginger hurtled down the stairs and he showed Leanne the gaping hole in the wall and the witch's den that lay beyond.

Leanne entered the room and immediately turned her eyes upwards. Alex was there all right; the broomstick had him firmly pinned to the ceiling!

"I'm here, Alex. We'll soon have you down, don't worry," she called confidently.

"Thanks, Leanne," said Alex, trying his best to be brave, but he couldn't stop his voice from shaking. "But

154

get me down as soon as you can, it's not very nice stuck up here."

" 'Course I will, Alex. Try not to worry, I'll get you down all right, but you must tell me everything that happened from start to finish, then I'll know what to do to make the broomstick release you, okay?"

And Alex, with the help of Ginger, told her everything that happened, right up to the time the broomstick had pinned him to the ceiling.

When Alex had finished talking, Leanne noticed more broomsticks neatly racked against the wall. She thought they looked a bit like billiard cues that had grown long ragged tails! They were arranged in two separate racks. Each rack had a notice printed above it: "Brooms programmed" said one, "Brooms not programmed" said the other.

Leanne observed that one of the programmed brooms was missing – evidently the one that had Alex pinned to the ceiling. She selected one of the other brooms from this rack and examined it closely. It had a small button embedded, almost flush with the surface of the handle, and on either side of this button, separated by a small horizontal line, two arrows were etched; one of the arrows pointed forward the other arrow pointed backwards. That button, she thought, must be the thing that makes the broomstick fly up or down.

"Okay, Alex, I'm coming – stand clear, Ginger!" Leanne straddled the broomstick, eased the button from the neutral to the forward position and the broomstick gently rose to the ceiling. Satisfied that she knew how to control the broomstick, Leanne moved the button carefully in the opposite direction, and this time the broomstick slowly descended. As soon as her feet touched the ground Leanne moved the flight button to the neutral position. The broomstick stopped quivering and lay perfectly still in her hands. Reassured that it was now completely harmless, Leanne replaced it in the rack and told Alex exactly what he had to do.

In no time at all he was safe on the ground and standing beside his big sister.

"Thanks, Leanne, that was easy. Now I know how that broomstick works, can I have another go and let Ginger have a go as well?"

"No, you can't, and neither can Ginger," Leanne snapped, and she marched both boys smartly out of the room.

"Right, upstairs, the pair of you," she said, "and wait for me, I've a few words to say to you before you go home, okay?"

The boys shuffled their feet, said they were sorry for causing all that trouble and shot off up the stairs to tell Laura how the broomsticks worked.

Leanne didn't instantly follow them; she wanted to see more of the witch's den. A slim black mobile phone lay on the table beside a pile of pamphlets. There were some heavily bound volumes lying higgledy-piggledy on the bookshelves, each one entitled *Spells – For Witches Only*. On another shelf were several purple-coloured bottles marked "MAGIC DUST (Read Instructions Carefully)".

Leanne had seen enough. She left the room and moved the coat peg in the hall back into its original position so that the panel in the wall closed again.

Upstairs she had a serious talk to Alex and Ginger and pointed out the dangers that lurked in the witch's den. They both promised faithfully they would never return to it again. When they left to go home Leanne said, "And don't tell anybody anything about what's happened here today, okay?"

"Okay, Leanne," they called back.

"And tidy up those pieces of rope as you go."

"Okay, Leanne."

"Do you think they'll keep their word, Laura?"

"Those two," sighed Laura, "No chance."

Laura was right. No sooner had Alex and Ginger arrived home than they reported to their parents exactly what had happened. No one believed them.

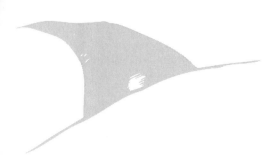

# CHAPTER SEVEN

## SINISTER HAPPENINGS
## AT THE TEA POT CAFÉ

The professor's nephew walked part way to the café with his uncle, Alison and Lindsey and then he left them to collect something from the workshop which would be required later at Red House Farm. He had escorted them part way to the café because he was concerned that the professor might be having problems with his artificial leg. But he needn't have worried, the professor easily out-paced them all!

Before his nephew left, Professor Klopstock told him not to bother about picking them up later, he was enjoying the journey up the hill on foot and it was on foot that he intended to make his way down.

Lindsey looked at her watch when they arrived at the café. It was exactly three o'clock.

Mrs Potts came to their table to serve them and immediately the professor stood and gave her a hug. "Hello, Rosie," he greeted her. "Why, you haven't changed a bit in over 50 years!"

Mrs Potts blushed. "Just listen to the blarney," she said, "I must have been only a kid the last time we saw one another."

Then Mrs Potts told them that she had just made a special strawberry flan and that everything was "on the house". The professor tried to get her to change her mind about that, but she wouldn't. Mrs Potts asked if they would all like to see some photographs taken of him in the old days.

They thought that this was a marvellous idea. The professor fingered his beard. "I don't think my beard was white then, Rosie, was it?"

Mrs Potts smiled and said politely, "You didn't have a beard then, Professor."

The professor laughed and insisted that from now on Rosie should call him by his first name. "Jules, Rosie," he said. "You must call me Jules."

"Come into the house then, Jules, you and the girls, after you've finished your tea. We can talk about old times and I'll show you the photographs, would you like to do that?"

"I'd be delighted," said the professor, and he stood up and gave Mrs Potts a bow; she replied by giving him a little curtsy, and then went into the house to get everything ready for their visit.

The professor and the girls tucked into the strawberry flan. It was absolutely delicious.

There were no other customers at the Tea Pot Café when they went into the house.

Lindsey saw Mrs Potts turn the sign on the door to "CAFÉ CLOSED" then she locked and bolted the door. Mrs Potts smiled and said, "There's nothing like a bit of privacy, is there? Go into the kitchen and make yourselves at home, the photograph album's there; it's lying on the table."

The professor, Lindsey and Alison trooped into the kitchen and gathered round the album. Before they had even opened it, a loud bang startled them all. They turned around to see that a trapdoor in the floor of the kitchen was open; a heavy stone slab lay close by. It must have been the heavy slab crashing down onto the stone floor of the kitchen that made so much noise.

Mrs Potts was standing by the open trapdoor and she wasn't smiling any more. Her expression was grim and she was pointing a gun at them. "It's loaded," she said.

"What's this, Rosie, is this some sort of a joke?" said the professor. "It's not funny, now put that dammed gun away and..."

He got no further; she fired a warning shot into the ceiling. "Shut your mouth, Professor Klopstock, or one of those girls will get the next bullet."

"But why, Rosie? Why are you doing this?"

"Why? Can't you guess? I'm doing it for money! Everything's done for money these days. Didn't you know that? It's money, money, money!" – and she shouted the word money more loudly every time she said it.

"But I thought you were comfortable here, Rosie, happily married with a profitable business?"

Mrs Potts sneered. "Well you thought wrong. I've never been happy in this place. I've slaved here since I was five. When my parents died I took it over and, yes, it was earning good money – that was, until the day I got married. My husband, Mr Potts, was a drinker and what he didn't spend on drink he gambled and lost on horses. When he died of drink recently, I was left with nothing but debt, mountains and mountains of debt. I've sold this place, you know. Oh yes, I'll be leaving soon, very soon. In fact the sooner the better, and very soon you'll find out the reason why."

160

"I'm sorry, I didn't know about all your troubles, Rosie..."

"Oh, don't worry about me, Professor, you're the way out of all my troubles – coming here today you've made me into a very rich woman, a very rich woman indeed."

"How? What do you mean?" The professor sounded quite bewildered by it all.

Mrs Potts waved her gun in the direction of the trapdoor. Her eyes were hard – "Go on, the lot of you, get down into that hole."

The professor hesitated. Mrs Potts fired a shot over Alison's head. "Down into the hole, I won't miss next time, I promise."

The girls were the first to go down the steps that led deep down into the cellar. They were both terrified and crying.

The professor followed, but two steps down he halted and said, "Who's paying you to do this, Rosie, and why?"

"Well now, just listen to him, folks, 'Who's paying you, Rosie, and why?' " she mimicked. "Just listen to Professor Know-it-all, the man who knows everything admitting he hasn't a clue. Well, I'll tell you the answer for nothing, Professor, it's because I've got plenty of money for you. I've sold you to the baddies that live under the hill, Professor – and for gold! Gold! Mountains of gold – and all of it paid in advance, what do you think about that? My debts paid off and plenty to spare, I can tell you. So goodbye Professor Klopstock and thank you." Then, bending down, she dragged the heavy stone lid back into place.

The professor and the girls found themselves in a large dark cellar. They held hands to try and lessen the fear. A few minutes passed and a door at the far end of the cellar opened and light came flooding in. Half a dozen almost dwarf-like creatures entered the cellar, they were fierce looking and each carried a long metal rod in his hand. They used the rods to prod their captives out of the cellar into the bright light and the passage beyond.

"Don't try anything foolish, girls," the professor said. "Those things they are carrying are electric probes. They can hurt, believe me."

The passage was high enough for the girls and their captors to move along easily, but the professor had to stoop. Age began to tell on him too, and he was glad when they reached the end of the passage that opened out into a large, well-lit cavern. Here they were herded into a cage that contained a few rough stone benches.

"Nice furniture," said the professor, sinking down onto one of them. "That's better," he said, and gave a little sigh of relief. The door slammed shut, the key turned in the lock and two guards stood outside to make sure they couldn't escape.

"Don't worry, girls," murmured the professor. "We'll be out of here in no time, you'll see." He yawned, stretched himself out on the bench, closed his eyes and fell fast asleep.

# CHAPTER EIGHT

## THE RESCUE

Alarmed by the sound of gunshots coming from café the little dish-washer woman, who had been on her way home, quickly turned back and looked through the kitchen window to see Mrs Potts forcing the professor and the girls down into the cellar. And minutes later, when she saw Mrs Potts leave the house carrying two large suitcases and get into a taxi, she knew that Mrs Potts would not be coming back.

The woman went to get help immediately. By taking a short cut down the slope by the café she soon reached the Sandstone Trail and she ran as fast as her short legs would carry her until she reached the stretch of the trail opposite Red House Farm. The slope down to the farm was steep, especially for such a short-legged person but she took a deep breath and plunged down the dark side of the hill, slipping, sliding and falling until at last she reached the broken fence around the farmyard.

Her clothes were torn, her face was scratched, she was muddy and dishevelled, when at last she fell exhausted on the floor of the upstairs room in which Laura and Leanne were talking to Eliot. A moment later, Jupiter arrived and said, "I f-ollowed her on the hill."

They sat the poor woman down and gave her a glass of water. "Not much English," she said, between sips.

"Take your time, take it easy," said Eliot, who was gently bathing the scratches on her face. "Looks like you've had a rough time."

Laura had an idea. "The helmets, Eliot," she said. "The helmets, they work, we've tried them."

Leanne produced two of the helmets, placed one of them on the woman's head and handed one to Eliot. He gave Laura a nod and she switched on the computer. All four of them stared intently at the screen to see if anything would happen. Almost instantly there was a reaction, the computer did what it had been designed to do and, within seconds, details of what had happened to the professor, Lindsey and Alison were flashed onto the screen. That was enough for Eliot; he took off his helmet and issued instructions. "You, Laura, you stay here with Leanne, if I haven't returned by five-thirty, the two of you – go home! Meantime, Juno will look after you 'til then. Have you got that, girls?"

The girls nodded.

"Come with me, Jupiter, we've got a job to do," said Eliot.

Jupiter led the way. The little woman took Eliot's hand and he helped her as she limped down the stairs. The girls heard the roar of the exhaust as he drove his car swiftly away.

Laura unplugged the helmets from the computer and put them away in their boxes. When that was done she began to make entries in the logbook. As she wrote, it occurred to her that the day hadn't been so boring after all and she made a note of that too!

She finished her writing and wandered around until she found some dusters. She handed one to Leanne.

"What's that for?" Leanne asked.

"Start dusting," said Laura, who was already busy with hers. "Keep our minds occupied, stop us from worrying about what's happening. Nothing like work for doing a thing like that."

"My mum doesn't have to wait until I look worried before she hands me a duster," said Leanne, and that made Laura laugh.

Time seemed to pass slowly. Laura looked at her watch; it was almost ten minutes to five.


At the Tea Pot Café, Jupiter had the door open and the trapdoor lid off within seconds. Eliot tried to persuade the little woman who had brought them there to stay where it was safe, in the kitchen. But she shook her head and kept a tight hold of his sleeve until he realized he wasn't going to go anywhere unless she went with him.

Eliot used his torch to find the door to the passage at the far end of the cellar. It was locked, but that didn't deter Jupiter, he had it open in a second and they were able to dispense with the torch light, because the passage they were entering was lit up as brightly as Blackpool in illumination week!

The professor's nephew was able to examine the walls as they moved down the passage; they were made up of different materials, layered, one layer on top of the other: rock, clay and sand. He saw a thin layer of white amongst the other layers in the wall, brushed a finger against it and tasted it on his tongue. It tasted like salt! He mentioned all of this to Jupiter. "Strat-igraphy," said Jupiter. "T-alk to the p-rofessor about it, he's the ar-chaeologist!"

They moved on, the light threw strange shadows on the walls giving the illusion of giant murals and then, in the distance, they saw the cage.

"Th-ey're in there," said Jupiter his binocular-like vision automatically adjusted to distance.

"Time for you to do your invisible trick then, Jupiter," said Eliot.

The guards couldn't believe what was happening, especially the guard with the key. His eyes boggled when he saw the key detach itself from his belt, float in the air and unlock the door of the cage. Then a stranger thing than that happened; he felt himself picked up by the scruff of the neck and tossed effortlessly into the cage. The same thing happened to the other guard and they sat together on the floor, looking completely bewildered, whilst the professor calmly led Lindsey and Alison out to freedom.

"Thank you, Jupiter," said the professor to empty space, "you got here even quicker than I expected!"

The door to the cage clanged shut, the key magically turned in the lock and the guards, who were now prisoners themselves, moaned with fear when they saw the key floating away in the air and landing an unreachable distance away from them.

The professor gave his nephew a big bear hug when he saw him, "Thanks, El, that was quick work, and the girls are fine. They were ever so brave. And Jupiter, of course, he was absolutely superb."

And they all crowded round Jupiter, who had now made himself visible. They congratulated him and told him what a great guy he was. Jupiter loved it.

Eliot told the professor about the important role the little woman from the café had played. The professor was fascinated; he looked at her closely. "And you've got a whole lot more to tell us, my dear, I can see by your eyes that you have."

The woman nodded her head as if she understood what he was saying.

"Best we get to know what it is then, and quickly," said the professor. "Look, El, first let's take the girls home, they've had enough for one day. And maybe they'll want to think twice before continuing with their watches? Don't blame them if they want to call it a day. What do you say, girls?" The girls insisted that they wanted to continue. After Eliot had dropped them off at home, he then went on to Red House with the others to relieve Laura and Leanne.

On the journey to Red House Farm, Jupiter told them that he estimated that there were only about a dozen of these tiny war-like creatures in the cave. He said he had seen them all huddled up, heads together as if in a meeting, not 50 paces away from the cage in which the professor and the girls had been held as prisoners. Jupiter was of the opinion that they were well armed and well trained warriors and were preparing for imminent action.

Leanne and Laura listened, aghast, while Eliot told them the story about what had happened at The Teapot Café on the hill. They couldn't believe that Mrs Potts was so evil.

Eliot looked at his watch. It was past six o'clock and he said to Leanne and Laura that it really was time for them to go home. They wanted to stay, but he insisted, and they understood why, when he told them that he didn't want their parents to be worried.

The professor thanked the girls and Eliot said that after he'd taken them home, he would call back later to pick him up. He said, "There's something I want you to explain to me, Uncle, perhaps you can tell me about it then?"

"What d'you want to ask me about, El? Tell me now, gives me time to think about it until you return."

"Stratigraphy," said Eliot, as he closed the door behind him.

When the sound of the car had faded away, the professor took out two thought transference helmets from their boxes, placed one on his head and offered the other one to the lady with the strange bright eyes. She took it, put it on and he gave her a dazzling smile as he switched on the screen and the computer. Allowing his thoughts to take over, he waited... "Now we can have a nice friendly little chat, just you and me, together. You start it off, tell me my dear lady, do you have a name?" All this came up as text on the screen without him saying a word. It was printed in two alphabets: the professor's familiar English alphabet and another, very unusual, almost Cyrillic-looking alphabet.

"Oonagh. Oonagh is my name." The message from her mind flashed across the screen in both languages.

"Thank you, Oonagh," came the professor's reply. "Is it okay if I record our conversation?"

"No objection to recording."

"Good." The professor pressed a switch and the recorder started working.

"Will you tell me where you come from, Oonagh, will you describe to me what it's like living there?"

"I come from the planet Petranova, that's the nearest translation into English of the name that I can think of. It is not of your galaxy. One side of our planet is very fertile, the other side is rich in minerals, but – dangerous." Oonagh somehow managed to put a stop on her thoughts at this stage and a cagey look came into her eyes. The professor

168

thought, "She doesn't want me to ask too many questions about Petranova."

"Thank you, Professor, you are correct." Oonagh's thoughts were texted upon the screen.

The professor couldn't help a little chuckle; he thought that the thought transference equipment designed by his nephew was good – almost too good!

"We possess more advanced, sophisticated equipment," was Oonagh's reply.

The professor nodded in acknowledgement and smiled, but her face remained impassive. He looked into her impenetrable eyes. "What's going on under the dark side of the hill, Oonagh? Can you tell me the story about that?"

Oonagh took another sip of water before she began to think about it.

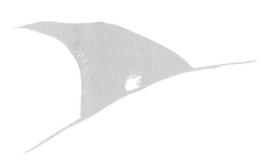

# CHAPTER NINE

## OONAGH'S STORY

Oohagh was still holding the glass of water in her hand as she began her story. "We were on a holiday flight when our spaceship was attacked and damaged by space pirates. Our pilot and navigation officer were killed, the flight engineer was injured and the navigation equipment became inoperable. The second pilot was also badly injured. We crashed on Tinsall Hill, which, as you now know, is almost completely hollow, and when our spaceship struck the ground the earth closed up around it and from then on we became invisible to the outside world. That was over 60 earth years ago. Your country was at war and Liverpool had a heavy air raid the night our spaceship crashed. Several landmines missed their target and fell in open space around Tinsall. Understandably, the noise our spaceship made when it crashed was thought to be one of those landmines. There was no damage to property or people. An investigation followed, but it was only perfunctory, it petered out quickly and the incident was soon forgotten."

"But those war-like people, who are they and how did they get onto the ship and what did they want with me?" asked the professor.

"They were infiltrators, undercover friends of the space pirates who mingled with the holidaymakers when everybody started to board. When the pirates attacked, they joined in to help them, but we outnumbered them, they were defeated and locked up.

"But when we crashed, they escaped with weapons taken from our store and gold bullion stolen from the spaceship's vault. They barricaded themselves in on one side of the hill; we, on the other side, were determined to defend ourselves against them whilst trying to repair the ship. It was a 'stand off' as you call it in America.

"Meantime, our flight engineer recovered from his injuries, and slowly, over the years, with the aid of some of the passengers, he worked on the spaceship until they had repaired it and made it serviceable once again. And the space pirates, who had been watching and waiting patiently for this to happen..."

"But surely, Oonagh," the professor's thoughts interrupted hers, "surely that was impossible. People grow old. By now everybody must have been too old to take part in all of these activities, after all it is over 60 years since the crash occurred and you came down on the hill?"

"Not too old for us, professor," Oonagh said, adjusting her headset, which was irritating her right ear. "Our life span is much greater than yours."

A thought message flashed up on the screen, in reply to one made by the professor. "No, sorry, professor, as far as your life span is concerned, we can't do anything to make a difference to that!" The professor laughed. Oonagh didn't. But the professor thought that he saw a slight change of light affect her piercing eyes.

"But what did they want, those little tough guys, when

they captured me?" The professor's thoughts were now on the screen.

"They paid Mrs Potts with some of the stolen gold so she would capture you and hand you over to them. They intended to use you as barter – your life and the girls' in exchange for..."

"I've got it." The professor slapped his tin leg with excitement and his thoughts came on the screen. "They were confident they could overpower you and when that happened, they wanted my nephew to check out the computers and then get Jupiter to join them, fly the spaceship so they could become space pirates and start all over again."

"Correct," came the answer from Oonagh. "Our leader, Uchtred, has asked me to try and arrange a meeting so he can persuade you to check the computers and get Jupiter to fly the ship and take the rest of us home."

"Oh, does he now? Well, I'm sure I can get my nephew to check out the computers, but as for the other thing, the Pentagon, maybe the President himself, will have to give his consent to that."

"But will you ask, will you try?" The question was quick and direct.

"Is it urgent?" the professor found himself thinking.

"Very urgent," came the reply. "Can't you see what a problem it would pose for your world if those space pirates took control of a sophisticated spaceship like ours? They would cause mayhem, do untold damage, cause wars, simply for the joy of it."

"I've got the message," the professor replied, looking worried. "Okay, okay, Oonagh, set up a meeting for me with your leader. I'll meet him tomorrow morning, ten o'clock, under the hill. You can take me there. I want to see the place for myself. Can you fix it?"

"Affirmative, consider it done," came the reply.

"Good, then meet me here at Red House Farm, tomorrow morning, nine-thirty, okay?"

"I'll be waiting for you, Professor."

"Excellent. My nephew, Eliot, will have returned with the car soon. I'm staying at the Boot Inn, just down the road from here. Can we drop you off somewhere, Oonagh?"

"No, not necessary, Professor. I will leave now to arrange for the meeting. See you here, tomorrow, nine-thirty in the morning."

When Oonagh left, the professor breathed a light sigh of contentment; as far as he was concerned the mystery of the dark side of the hill had already been solved and strangely, though her name meant "obscure" Oonagh was the one who had enlightened him.

The professor picked up the phone and within seconds he was talking to someone very important in the Pentagon.

He heard the sound of his nephew's car arriving as he put the phone down. He was glad to hear it. Although he was fit, it had been a very full day for someone who was getting on a bit in years. The professor yawned. He was looking forward to a nice warm meal and then early to bed at the Boot.

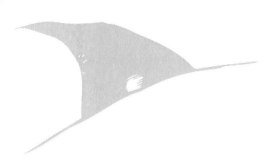

# CHAPTER TEN

## WITCH EASTLY USES HER WMP

Far away in her prison cell, Mrs Eastly was totally unaware that her witch's den at Red House Farm no longer remained a secret.

Mrs Eastly was bored. "Lights out" had sounded over an hour ago but she couldn't sleep. She was pacing up and down her cell in the gloom when she caught sight of the witch's mobile phone that lay on the locker next to her bed.

For the want of something to do, she picked up the phone and pressed a button. "Red Leader, Red Leader, Bertha Eastly calling, over."

"Sister Eastly from Witches Control Centre, you are transmitting on an emergency channel. Clear the channel immediately." The controller in the Centre sounded annoyed. Sister Eastly hastily obeyed the controller's command.

Mrs Eastly had forgotten what the function of the Witches Control Centre was, but she remembered enough to know that she shouldn't be broadcasting on an emergency channel. She studied the numbers on the WMP again, found the number she should have pressed in the first instance, stabbed at it with a bony finger and repeated her call to Red Leader. Red Leader responded immediately in a voice that was bright and cheerful. "Red Leader to Mrs Eastly, read you loud and clear. Pass your message, over."

Mrs Eastly had already had enough of this "Roger, Wilco, over and out" stuff. It annoyed her. But keeping a civil tongue in her head, she asked Red Leader if she would kindly pop over and see her just as soon as she found it convenient.

"Wilco, Roger, over and out," came Red Leader's bright reply. Mrs Eastly scowled, flung the WMP on the locker and lay on the bed to wait.

She didn't have to wait very long, ten minutes at the most, and then came a sharp rat-a-tat-tat on the window pane. Mrs Eastly turned her head on the pillow and in the moonlight she saw two familiar blob-like faces, bobbing up and down, outside. It was Red Leader and Red One. Mrs Eastly was pleased to see them; she got out of the bed and went over to have a chat. Red Leader greeted her by saying, "Who's been a naughty girl, then, calling on the emergency channel?" She raised a gloved hand and wagged a finger. "Naughty, naughty! she said.

Mrs Eastly grimaced, but making her voice sound as pleasant as she possibly could, said, "Just wanted to thank you for those infra-red photos you took at Red House Farm. But I couldn't make out what this is," and she pointed to something on the photograph.

"Oh yes, I wondered what that was myself, so I had it blown up," said Red Leader. "And believe it or not, Sister Bertha, that thing you're looking at is a robot. Yes – a robot! Something strange is happening on Tinsall Hill and the robots and people occupying Red House Farm

175

all seem to be involved in whatever it is that's going on there."

"And children as well," said Red One. "Don't forget we saw children as well."

"Children! Children! Did you say children? What sort of children?" Mrs Eastly screamed.

"Young girls," said Red One.

"Young girls are they? Well, I can guess who they are. Well, the good news is they won't have to wait much longer before they get to see me again. They told me today I'm going to get out of prison early because of my good behaviour. It can't come too soon, either. I've been waiting for that to happen so I can pay those children back for what they did to me."

Red Leader and Red One looked at one another in amazement when they heard Mrs Eastly muttering threats about what she would do to the girls when she was released from prison, how she would change them into cockroaches or toads or something even more horrible. Red Leader and Red One put their heads together and began to whisper.

Mrs Eastly saw them. "What are you two whispering about?" she demanded. "Come on, Red Leader, out with it!"

"We were just saying, Mrs Eastly, that if you start putting spells on people the moment you get out of prison, you'll make yourself unpopular with our new leader, very unpopular indeed."

"New leader! New leader! What's all this about a new leader? I've heard nothing about a new leader. There has to be an election held in order to choose a new leader."

Red One replied, "But there has been an election, Mrs Eastly. You weren't allowed to vote because you were in prison, and it was a landslide victory for the new leader."

"And our new leader is determined to change our image," said Red Leader. "She thinks that the public's perception of witches and their behaviour in general is poor. She's out to change all that by creating a New Order. She says the Old Order has to go."

The news was all too much for Mrs Eastly – she was averse to change – she wanted things to stay exactly as they were. Feeling weak, she left the window and sat on the edge of her bed and called out aloud, "And who is this new leader, the one who is going to change everything, does this new leader have a name?"

"Of course she has a name," said Red Leader. "It's Sister Mabel, our commandant – your cousin – Mrs Eastly, she's been voted in as our new leader."

Stunned by the news, Mrs Eastly fell back on her bed and closed her eyes. She lay still; her visitors thought she had fallen asleep.

Red Leader spoke through her microphone to Red One, "Red One, prepare for high-speed run back to base, over."

"Red Leader," acknowledged Red One.

"Red One from Red Leader, "Go! Go! Tally-ho!"

And the two witches, astride their high-speed broomsticks, disappeared into the night sky before Mrs Eastly could even whisper goodbye.

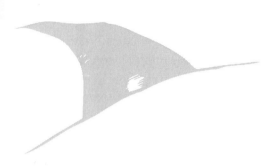

# CHAPTER ELEVEN

## THE FINAL ASSAULT

The morning after Lindsey and Alison and he had been rescued from the space pirates, the professor was not in the least bit surprised to find that all the Ponyteers had turned up early at Red House Farm. Parents and grandparents, in the case of Laura, had phoned him the night before to tell him they had given in to the demands of the children who wanted to see the investigation through to the end. Alex and Ginger insisted that in the interests of safety they should escort the girls to Red House Farm and in the interests of peace and harmony, the girls accepted their kind offer.

Oonagh had arrived before any of them and she tugged at the professor's sleeve to make it plain that she had something important to tell him. Laura immediately produced the special headgear so they could see on the screen what it was that she had to say.

When the professor and Oonagh donned their helmets, Leanne switched on the computer and Oonagh's thought messages immediately began to appear. Her messages were short and to the point. Uchtred was convinced that the space pirates, having failed to capture the professor, would now be preparing to make one last major attempt to gain control of the spaceship. A final cry for help from Uchtred appeared on the screen. It was a heart-rending plea and the professor made up his mind to give him all the help that he could.

Eliot came into the room and the professor told him of his immediate plans. "I'm going with Oonagh and Jupiter, we're going into the hill to try and sort things out. Keep an eye on the screen, El. You never know, we may require some help ourselves. Okay?"

"Okay, I'll keep watch. And you, Jules, take care. Promise. And shout if you need any help."

"Do my best, El, don't worry." He spoke to the girls who were busy storing the special headgear away. "Now, girls, I've read your report about Alex and Ginger and what took place in Mrs Eastly's den. And it's well done to Alex and Ginger, and particularly well done to Leanne for getting Alex down from the ceiling. But what I want you to do now is to take Juno down into the witch's den and get her to scan every page in every spell book and every scrap of paper that you can find. You'll be amazed how quickly Juno works, she'll have every single item scanned and stored in her data banks before you can say 'hocus-pocus'."

Alex and Ginger laughed; hocus-pocus sounded funny. They'd never heard that word before. But they decided that they would wait until the professor had left them before asking Leanne if she knew what it meant.

The professor said a final goodbye and departed with Oonagh and Jupiter.

Oonagh led the way, the professor and Jupiter followed. The professor's metal leg squeaked in protest when it was tested by the steepness of the hill.

179

Oonagh took out from a pocket in her skirt something that looked like a remote control device, something similar to the type drivers use to open and close their car doors. She pointed it at a specific spot on the hill, pressed a button and a scorched brown grass door, supported on a metal frame, came sliding open. As soon as they crossed the threshold, the door closed behind them, and they descended a steep stairway that seemed to have no ending.

Eventually they reached the bottom of the steps where they were met by two armed guards who escorted them to meet Uchtred. These guards were very different to the war-like looking creatures that had threatened the professor, Lindsey and Alison with electric probes and forced them into a cage. They were small in stature, like the space pirates, but there the resemblance ended; the faces of these people were gentle and their manner, friendly.

The professor noted that the guards handled their weapons clumsily, and he couldn't help thinking, "If it comes to battle and the rest of 'em are like this, then heaven help them. They are not fighters."

Uchtred came to meet the professor with outstretched arms, palms open towards them. It was Uchtred's way of bidding his guests welcome, whilst demonstrating that he was unarmed.

Recognising this outward sign of peace, the professor responded in similar fashion. Then someone handed him a piece of headgear, he put it on and looked for the wires leading to the computer to which it should have been attached. There weren't any wires to be seen and no computer – nothing!

He felt something being strapped to his wrist. At first glance it looked like an oversized wristwatch, but a closer inspection showed it to be more like a small television screen. There was a switch on the side of the screen and he was invited to switch it on. Immediately, words appeared on the screen. "Greetings, and welcome from the people of Petranova, Professor, and thank you for your kind offer to help."

Once again the professor looked for the power leads and the computer, but there were none to be seen. He read the message that came up for him to read. "There are no connecting wires, Professor, your headset contains all the necessary electronic remote control equipment which links it to the main computer in the spaceship. The main computer interprets and analyses your thoughts, relays them to me, my answers are then translated into your language and shown to you on the screen. It's a two-way device, enabling us to communicate with one another, even though we do not speak the same language."

"Phew! My nephew's got a bit of work to do, to catch up with this lot," thought the professor.

"Yes," came back the answer, "we estimate that it will take approximately 15 more earth years before your scientists produce equipment of this advanced standard. But come, Professor, let me show you round our world, the world we have lived and worked in for over 60 earth years."

First, Uchtred showed the professor several small reservoirs; all were full of crystal clear water. Uchtred explained that the water from the surface of the hill had filtered down through layers of sand and gravel which had purified it. Water surplus to requirements was drained off and allowed to run down the hill outside, where it eventually it found its way into a small muddy stream that ran through a field close to Red House Farm. The professor smiled when he saw that bit of news come up on his screen.

Obviously the muddy stream to which Uchtred referred was the stream out of which, Lindsey's so called monsters from the deep had emerged. A message on his screen read, "Monsters of the deep? Regret, unable to interpret. Unable to interpret..." The professor thought, "Well, nothing in this world is perfect, is it?" He looked at the screen on his wrist, there was no reply, the screen was completely blank!

Uchtred took a small yellow pill from a pouch that was fastened to the belt at his waist. "This will sustain me as food for seven earth days," the message said as he swallowed it. "Now follow me, Professor, I have something of interest to show you."

He led the party across the cave towards the heavily curtained entrance of another cavern. Uchtred pulled the curtain aside. It took a few moments for their eyes to adjust to the gloom, then the leader from Petranova took them inside and pointed to trays and trays of something growing in the dark. They were mushrooms! Here was a mushroom farm! The sheer size of it made the professor gasp. "My people are very fond of this product," said Uchtred, mildly.

Back in the main cavern and the brilliant lighting, the professor was able to take a good look at Uchtred. The man appeared younger than 40 and yet his spaceship had crashed over 60 years ago; it didn't seem to make sense.

The professor's thoughts were answered. "The average life span in Petranova is 600 earth years. I am 200 earth years old." The screen went blank again. It was then that the professor realized that Uchtred knew how to delete his own thoughts when he wished to change the subject.

After a few minutes the screen on the professor's wrist lit up again and a new message appeared. "Now perhaps you will allow me to take you and Jupiter to see the spaceship, it's repaired and almost ready for launch. All we need now is for your nephew to check our computers and your permission granted for Jupiter to take over the controls."

Jupiter wasn't wearing any special headgear, although he knew perfectly well what was going on. Up to now he'd been quiet, but the idea of being given an opportunity to fly a spaceship triggered off his most enthusiastic response, "H-ey, Uchtred. Cool, man, real cool." And when he actually saw the spaceship his red light flashed. "It w-ould be a p-leasure to fly this b-aby. Yeah!"

And for the first time that day, the professor saw Uchtred show his teeth in a smile! When the professor saw the sleek design of the spaceship, his eyes opened wide. It was not overly large but he guessed that it could carry at least 100 passengers. "Correct!" the answer came onto his screen.

He tried to guess the speed of the ship. The answer that came back was not expressed in miles per hour. "Almost the speed of light," were the words he saw on his screen. The professor gasped, almost 186,000 earth miles per second, now that was really travelling." The professor felt humble, he couldn't design a spaceship to compete with this, it was way beyond his capabilities. "Another 20 years, perhaps?" was the reply he saw on his display unit!

Suddenly, their conversation was abruptly halted by the warning sound of alarm bells ringing and a loud message was repeatedly issued over the underground broadcast system. The professor looked at his wrist to see if the warning had been translated for him. "Under enemy attack, under enemy attack," the message read. "All defence units to sector one!"

"So it's started then..." The professor was talking to Jupiter when Uchtred interrupted and indicated they should follow him to sector one.

Arriving there, the professor and Jupiter surveyed the scene of battle and were not impressed by what they saw. There were three main lines of defence, but already the defenders were starting to waver. Uchtred's people were peaceful folk who hated fighting and it was clear to the professor and Jupiter they didn't even know how to use their weapons. "It's no contest," he said, "its like fighting machine guns with bows and arrows."

"Want me to f-ix it?" asked Jupiter, not liking what he saw.

"The space pirates are operating in four groups of three. There are only twelve of them, see?" said the professor, pointing out their positions. "Yes, go in, Jupiter, bang a few heads and fix it."

Jupiter vanished and one by one pirates' heads collided with each other and weapons flying out of pirates' hands mysteriously disappeared. Within minutes the battle was over and, convinced they were being attacked by demons, the space pirates fled to seek out Uchtred. Finding him, they fell on their knees and pleaded for his protection. Uchtred obliged by locking them up in the same cage from which they had escaped over 60 years ago. Since then the cage had been well repaired and strengthened. The prisoners didn't mind that at all; the stronger the cage was to keep them in, the stronger it must be to keep those demons out!

Uchtred viewed his wrist screen again. There was a message from the professor. "We'll leave you now, Uchtred. It's all over. Peace at last for you. How do you feel about that?"

Uchtred replied, "After 60 years of fighting we can become 'gentle people' again, thanks to you and Jupiter, Professor."

The professor said that Eliot would be along next morning to start checking the computers, but that it might

184

take a few days before they heard from America. "We have to get permission for Jupiter to man the spaceship. There's so much to consider and you may have to be patient a while longer."

Uchtred bowed towards him and with a gentle expression on his face, sent his message, "Patience we have in abundance, Professor, we have nurtured 60 earth years of patience under the dark side of the hill. If we have to spend a few days more waiting, we know it will be amongst friends. Could our time be spent better than that?" The professor gave Uchtred the thumbs up sign and was rewarded with one of Uchtred's rare smiles.

They arranged to exchange news through Oonagh. Bidding one another farewell, Oonagh accompanied Jupiter and the professor out of the hill. Before they parted company she agreed that she would be at Red House Farm at midday daily until everything had been settled.

The professor looked over his shoulder as he walked with Jupiter down the hill to Red House Farm, but there was nothing to see, Oonagh had disappeared and the door to the hill had closed.

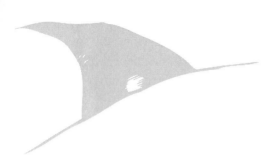

# CHAPTER TWELVE

## RETURN TO PETRANOVA

The news about what had happened on the dark side of the hill flashed round the village of Tinsall like wildfire and at last word came from America to say that Jupiter had been given permission to fly the "gentle people" back to Petranova. It was the President himself who gave the written order and a top-ranking air force general brought it to Tinsall and read it to the villagers who had turned out in force to greet him.

Mr Gribe, the local newspaper reporter, printed the story in the Chester People's Daily and overnight the City of Chester became the most important city in the world. As for Mr Gribe, he basked in the glory of being the world's most important newspaper reporter and it lasted for almost a week!

Journalists from newspapers, television, radio and the film industry all flooded into Chester. They sought out the American air force general who told them the reason for his stay in England and they photographed the President's letter. The President's permission for Jupiter to fly the "gentle people" back to Petranova on humanitarian grounds was particularly well received.

The media besieged the professor and his nephew, and details of Eliot's "mikes on spikes" that had enabled him to hear Jupiter's victorious underground battle against the space pirates were published in many technical journals. Mr Gribe, who had written last year about Alison's accident and rescue in the local Chester paper, repeated the story to a hungry press and immediately the Ponyteers became world famous too!

The councillors and Mayor of Chester were very impressed when they learned about the long struggle that Uchtred and his people had endured under Tinsall Hill and they decided to honour him with a banquet to take place in the Town Hall on the night before his departure to Petranova. The professor, his nephew, and the American air force general sat alongside Uchtred at the table reserved for the guests of honour.

The banquet was a great success, scientists and high-ranking representatives from many countries had been invited; there were no refusals. Everyone wanted to meet Uchtred and witness his departure in the spaceship the following morning.

Every hotel in the city was full.

When the banquet was over, the professor accompanied the air force general back to Tinsall, where he had invited him to be his guest at the Boot Inn.

They stood for a while in the cool night air, enjoying the scent of roses and honeysuckle that grew up the old sandstone walls of the inn. A full moon illuminated the sky, shining its bright, silvery light on Tinsall Hill, but one dark patch remained dark no matter how brightly the moon tried to change it. And when the professor pointed to this area and told the general all about it, his friend could scarcely believe that such a place as the dark side of the hill could exist in the midst of so much beauty.

They decided it was time for bed. It had been a very long and busy day, and the professor, in particular, was feeling very tired. As he turned to open the door of the inn he saw the general's jaw drop.

"Look, Jules, S-s-see that?" the general stammered, pointing up at the clear sky. "See that, Jules?"

The professor looked and there, silhouetted against the moon, was Red Leader followed by the rest of her team, heading south on a high-speed exercise. The professor saw a few delicate wisps of cloud drifting across the moon and pretended that was the scene the general was referring to. "Yes, very picturesque," he remarked. How could he explain Mrs Eastly to the general or describe the secrets of Red House Farm? How could he expect his friend, an air force general, to imagine being pinned to the ceiling by a broomstick that had got out of control?

Fortunately the general suddenly looked more tired than the professor. "Think I'll turn in now, Jules, jet lag you know."

Jules was glad to say goodnight.

They asked to be called at seven o'clock the next morning, to give themselves plenty of time to get ready for the spaceship's departure. The take-off was scheduled for ten.

As early as six o'clock next morning the village of Tinsall was wide-awake and buzzing with excitement. Word had got around about take-off time and already a steady stream of sightseers were setting out to seek a vantage point on the hill.

Eliot and Jupiter were still working on the spacecraft and it wasn't until nine o'clock in the morning that Eliot was satisfied the computers were fully operational and Jupiter had finally familiarised himself with the controls. When it

188

was all over and done with, Jupiter turned to Eliot, "C-ool man, c-ool. Hey, El, high f-ive! High Five!" and flesh and metal met together to mark the high point of their success.

The Ponyteers, and Alex and Ginger Tomkins, were in the observation room at Red House Farm together with their parents and grandparents. "Wish we were going with them," Alex and Ginger said, and at least one of the girls said she wouldn't mind going as well.

"Wait until Jupiter comes back first. Let's hear what he says about Petranova before you make hasty decisions like that," said Alex's dad.

"That's right, Chris," said Alex's granddad and turning to Alex, he said, "You want to listen to your dad, Alex – he always talks sense."

On comfortable chairs arranged on a specially constructed platform, close to the take-off point, the professor and the American air force general sat with the mayor and his wife, the Bishop of Chester, the local MP and several local parish councillors.

Two military photographers, one British, the other American, clicked away with their cameras, they were the only people allowed to go near the platform except for Constable Pearson from the village. Somehow his broad, cheerful smile contributed a spirit of carnival to the scene.

Scattered among the crowd who were watching outside the enclosed area were a sprinkling of serious looking security men in dark suits and wearing dark glasses. They communicated with one another via microphones hidden under the lapels of their jackets and they never seemed to stop talking.

At nine-fifteen a door in Tinsall Hill opened and a piece of apparatus resembling a huge tuning fork emerged, carrying the spacecraft on its twin booms. The crowd gasped and gaped when they saw it and some of them made a move down the hill to get a closer look, but the police and security men ordered them back and warned them not to try to get any closer.

At nine-twenty the door of the spaceship opened, steps automatically unfolded and were lowered to the ground. In groups of ten the "gentle people" emerged from the hill and began to climb the steps up to the ship. As they reached the door of the spaceship, the last one of each group turned and waved to the crowd and the crowd roared and waved back in response.

The last person to enter the spacecraft was Uchtred. At the top of the steps he, too, turned to face the crowd, and after opening his arms wide to their fullest extent, he then drew them slowly towards his body and it seemed as if this gesture was his way of enfolding the whole human race in a loving embrace. The crowd called and cheered until he disappeared into the spaceship.

Jupiter stopped three times as he climbed the steps to turn and wave to the crowd. Each time the swell of the applause from the crowd grew louder. "He loves it," whispered Eliot to his uncle.

"I know," replied Professor Klopstock. "You helped to make him, El. There's something of both of us in him. How do you feel about that?"

Jupiter paused at the top of the steps to give a final wave before entering the spaceship. The steps retracted and the door of the spaceship closed behind him and at the same time all the secret doors closed in the hill. The time was now nine fifty-five am.

A strange hush came over the crowd as they waited for take-off.

At precisely ten o'clock the Ponyteers watched as the spaceship, with only a whisper of sound, lifted slowly off the twin booms, hovered for a second and then began to make the slow climbing turn of its ascent.

Down below the cameras were clicking away like crazy. "Look at him," cried Eliot, "cheeky devil's going to do a farewell circuit first."

And much to the photographers' delight that's what Jupiter did. The spaceship passed very close to the observation room in Red House Farm where it stopped climbing and hovered while everyone in the room waved wildly to Jupiter, who thrilled them all by waving back. The spaceship sped off in the direction of Chester where it slowed down and hovered over the Cross that stood at the heart of the city. People shopping on The Rows leaned over the railings, risking injury to look skywards to get a good view. Walkers on the city walls who caught a glimpse of the spaceship stopped to reflect on the way life had changed since the Romans occupied their city!

In the observation room at Red House Farm, the Ponyteers were the first to see the change that was beginning to take place on Tinsall Hill. The brown dead patch of the dark side of the hill was slowly being transformed; shoots of fresh green grass were springing up and spreading across the whole of the area. Rose bushes grew as if by magic, their red hips shining like rubies in the late summer sun and blackberry bushes, laden with fruit, trailed their rambling branches along the ground. There were damson trees galore, dripping with purple fruit, ripened and swollen, ready to be boiled in the pot and made into jam!

But where did it all come from, all this profusion? The Ponyteers didn't know why or how it had happened, neither did their parents or grandparents. They shook their heads and said it was a miracle.

Lindsey whispered softly, "I think it looks like the picture of Switzerland hanging in Grandma's cottage," and everyone who had seen the picture agreed that Lindsey was right.

So, from then on they decided to call that part of Tinsall Hill by a new name. They named it "Little Switzerland" and that is the name the villagers call it to this day.